Elise

Doug Witt

Copyright © 2014 by Doug Witt.

Library of Congress Control Number:	2014913812
ISBN: Hardcover	978-1-4990-5834-5
Softcover	978-1-4990-5835-2
eBook	978-1-4990-5833-8

All rights reserved. No part of this book may be reproduced or transmitted in any form or by any means, electronic or mechanical, including photocopying, recording, or by any information storage and retrieval system, without permission in writing from the copyright owner.

This is a work of fiction. Names, characters, places and incidents either are the product of the author's imagination or are used fictitiously, and any resemblance to any actual persons, living or dead, events, or locales is entirely coincidental.

Any people depicted in stock imagery provided by Thinkstock are models, and such images are being used for illustrative purposes only.
Certain stock imagery © Thinkstock.

This book was printed in the United States of America.

Rev. date: 08/15/2014

Contact Doug at doug.witt@thinktocope.com

To order additional copies of this book, contact:
Xlibris LLC
1-888-795-4274
www.Xlibris.com
Orders@Xlibris.com
552999

CONTENTS

Dedication 7

Prologue 9

Chapter 1   What my Dad does 11

Chapter 2   Labor Day Tuesday 1976 13

Chapter 3   Wednesday 16

Chapter 4   Thursday 19

Chapter 5   Saturday afternoon game 23

Chapter 6   Sunday—Humility:
            It is about Perspective and Acceptance 25

Chapter 7   Monday—Discipline:
            It is about Visualization and Practice 42

Chapter 8   Tuesday—Faith: It is about Belief and Trust 51

Chapter 9   Piano Practice—Session 1 59

Chapter 10 Wednesday—Courage:
            It is about Choice and Change 62

Chapter 11 Thursday—Optimism:
            It is about Attitude and Hope 70

Chapter 12 Piano Practice—Session 2 75

Chapter 13 Friday—Kindness:
            It is about Patience and Gentleness 79

Chapter 14	Saturday—Charity: It is about Sharing and Forgiving............................85
Chapter 15	Game Time..89
Chapter 16	Everyday—Presence: It is about Breathing and Awareness......................91
Chapter 17	Playbook 103
Chapter 18	Emotional Architect....................................114
Chapter 19	Elise Matthews...122
Chapter 20	Ryan Edwards 131
Chapter 21	Review..141
Chapter 22	Starfish Story...144
Chapter 23	Reflection 146
Chapter 24	Man in Motion—Eight Days a Week.........148
Chapter 25	Locker Room..150
Chapter 26	Game on 153
Chapter 27	Homecoming 157
Chapter 28	Piano Practice – Session 3 160
Chapter 29	December Recital 164
Chapter 30	Graduation 168
Chapter 31	Back at Matthew's Class 172

Epilogue..*181*

Dedicated to my wife

Written for my boys

PROLOGUE

"If you have an important point to make, don't try to be subtle or clever. Use a pile driver. Hit the point once. Then come back and hit it again. Then hit it a third time—a tremendous whack."

Winston Churchill

CHAPTER 1

WHAT MY DAD DOES

> "The happiness of your life depends upon the quality of your thoughts."
>
> Marcus Aurelius

Ryan Edwards arrived at the elementary school that October Monday morning in 2008, driving his car into the first visitor's parking spot. As he turned off the engine, he reviewed again what he would say at his son's third grade "What my Dad does" talk that was to begin in fifteen minutes. He gathered his things and walked to the front entrance of the school. Having turned off his BlackBerry, he was free from the responsibilities of his business for the next thirty minutes. What a blessing such a small gift could be.

In the hallway his nine-year-old son, Matthew, was proudly waiting. "Come on, Dad," Matthew exclaimed, "everyone is waiting." As Matthew took his dad's hand and led him into the classroom, Ryan began to wonder where this talk was going to start, where it was going to go, and where it was going to end.

Miss Wright, Matthew's teacher, announced, "Children, Mr. Edwards has arrived. Please take your seats." She shook Ryan's hand and gestured for Ryan to lean back against her desk. Positioned in the front of the classroom, Ryan Edwards could address the twenty students in Matt's class.

Matt then rose from his seat, walked to the front, hesitated, and began, "This is my dad, Ryan Edwards. He is forty-nine years old. Today he will talk about what he does all day when he is not at home with my mom and my three brothers, and of course, with me."

Matt then walked back to his seat and sat down. The room was ever so quiet. Not easily ruffled, Ryan himself paused, not really sure of where to start. He knew that the business world wasn't going to be particularly exciting to a score of nine-year-old boys and girls. He was neither a rock star, nor a movie star, nor a professional athlete. He felt a little sheepish about describing who he was in a way that would be interesting to twenty third-graders.

Breaking the heavy silence, Ryan began to speak, "Thank you, Matt. Good morning, boys and girls. I am Ryan Edwards, Matt's dad." Ryan realized how nervous he was, having just repeated what Matt had said. "Thank you for inviting me to spend a few minutes with your third-grade class today." Although quite accomplished in public speaking forums, Ryan continued his filler words of introduction, still not quite sure where he was going. As he rambled on without any particular direction, he caught the eye of Miss Wright, Matt's teacher. Quite attractive, in her early thirties, Elizabeth Wright smiled and nodded with encouragement in a way he hadn't seen for thirty-two years, not since his senior year in high school. Not since music class with his teacher Elise Matthews . . .

CHAPTER 2

LABOR DAY TUESDAY 1976

"It's not the critic who counts, not the man who points out how the strong man stumbled, or where the doer of deeds could have done them better. The credit belongs to the man who is actually in the arena; whose face is marred by dust, sweat and blood; who strives valiantly; who errs and comes short again and again; who knows the great enthusiasms, the great devotions and spends himself in a worthy cause; who at the best knows in the end the triumph of high achievement, and who at the worst, if he fails, at least fails while daring greatly, so that his place will never be with those cold and timid souls who know neither victory nor defeat."
                                    Theodore Roosevelt

Ryan Edwards was the star quarterback of the Fairfield High School football team. It was September 5, the Tuesday after Labor Day, of his senior year, and there were high expectations for the accomplished quarterback, who had a promising college career ahead of him. Ryan was extremely good-looking—6'1" in height, brown hair, blue eyes, and a smile that softened the consequences of most any trouble Ryan found himself in. Ryan was popular, had many friends, and the girls were always talking about him. Ryan Edwards, by all accounts of his peers and teachers, had it made. He could do whatever he wanted, and he did. His arrogant swagger was both disgusting and attractive at the same time.

On this first day of school at Fairfield High, Ryan was feeling as confident as ever. He knew he would have a very good season in football, that the college recruiters would lavish him with interest, and that he would have full scholarship offers as quarterback to several top state schools—and possibly to even an Ivy League or two.

Ryan and his classmates were collecting their class schedules and attending fifteen-minute introductory sessions with each teacher, picking up a sense for what was expected in each class. In Ryan's mind this year was all about football anyway. He was quick to translate how easy each class would be and how many corners he could cut.

Ryan went from class to class—English, Spanish, calculus, history, physics—and was coming up to his last session, music, which was the only thing keeping him from the football field and practice. The students entered Room 101 in the music building and found Miss Matthews writing some instructions on the board as they took their seats.

When the bell rang indicating class had begun, Elise Matthews turned to the class. She introduced herself, "Good morning and welcome. My name is Elise Matthews, and I will be your music teacher this semester. Coming to Fairfield as a new teacher is very exciting for me. I hope you will share in my excitement as you develop your very own appreciation for music during this semester."

Elise Matthews was a knockout—thirty-one years old, single, blonde, blue-eyed, athletic, and a wonderful figure—music class was going to be all right in Ryan's mind. The summary highlights of the music curriculum for the semester were lost on Ryan as he stared at Elise Matthews with his cocky, evaluative smile. Miss Matthews then caught his attention saying, "Confucius said, 'I hear and I forget. I see and I remember. I do and I understand.'" Elise continued, "In keeping with that idea, each of you will choose an instrument for the semester, learn the fundamentals of playing that instrument, and perform a piece at a recital at the end of the semester before Christmas."

There was dead silence in the room. You could have heard a pin drop. Music had always been the class where you could go to take a nap. Mrs. Rockefeller, the previous music teacher for forty years, was very nice but quite old; everyone loved her class because you didn't have to do anything. If you weren't sleeping through it, you could do your math or science in class that you should have done the night before. It was a bonus study hall for the lazy.

Miss Matthews continued, "I ask that each of you determine this evening the instrument you wish to learn. Tomorrow we will begin a plan for your instruction. I have identified several teachers who will give you lessons at least once a week on the saxophone, violin, cello, trumpet, and piano. Since my training is on the piano, I will teach those of you who choose it."

Ryan was about to get sick. Music was supposed to be a joke—no expectations, no work, no hassles, and one full academic point toward graduation. This was not the way it was supposed to be. Furthermore, Ryan had no interest whatsoever in music, unless it was the latest rock stars like Aerosmith, The Rolling Stones, or Led Zeppelin. There was no way he would play the cello, violin, saxophone, or trumpet. He would lose his instrument within the first week.

Reflecting on the fact that his mother played the piano and that there was a piano at home, Ryan decided on the piano. As for Miss Matthews, he would charm her. He would soften her tough exterior, and perhaps he would even talk his way out of having to learn any music, let alone perform in the recital.

The bell rang. "Class dismissed," Elise Matthews exclaimed. "Please choose your instrument by this time tomorrow in class."

CHAPTER 3

WEDNESDAY

"Faith is different from proof; the latter is human, the former is a Gift from God."

Blaise Pascal

The next day at music class Ryan wrote piano on the instrument selection sheet. Ryan Edwards always looked good. He had to for himself and for his own self-esteem, though he was unconscious of that reality. He was unaware how much he needed to pump himself up. He wore Top-Siders, khaki pants, and blue-and-white-checked button-down shirt. Ryan Edwards was always on camera.

Miss Matthews collected all of the students' selection sheets and ordered them in groups according to instrument. "Very well," she began, "all those who selected the saxophone please go to room 105. Those of you who chose the violin go to room 107, the cello—room 109, the trumpet—room 111. Those of you who are interested in the piano, please stay here." Elise Matthews looked stunning again. She had an air of strength and fragility at the same time. Her manner was precise yet delicate too. One could sense that she once was invincible but somehow had been knocked down and emotionally injured. It was her human vulnerability matched with her strength that was so attractive.

As the students gathered their belongings to proceed to their appropriate rooms, Ryan began to feel a little uneasy. His friend Robbie, the star wide receiver, leaned over on the way out saying, "Good luck, Ryan." Everybody was getting up and leaving the room—everyone that is except for Ryan Edwards. Nobody had selected piano except for Ryan.

Ryan sat frozen. What was he thinking? The talk the evening before was that Elise Matthews was a witch—albeit a very attractive one—and that anyone taking up the piano under her instruction should have his head examined. Clearly Ryan was now wondering if he had miscalculated.

As the room emptied except for Ryan Edwards and Elise Matthews, the silence was deafening. Elise began, "Well, aren't you the brave one. In addition to regular class, you will be required to have a thirty-minute piano lesson each week under my direction. Please think about some suitable times for your lessons, and we will set a regular schedule after our first session tomorrow at 7:00 a.m. That is the only time I have available this week, and I want you to get a fast start on this one."

At this point Ryan could no longer help himself, "You know, Miss Matthews, this isn't the way music class is typically taught at Fairfield for seniors. And normally, I am still asleep at 7:00 a.m."

To which Elise Matthews replied, "You know, Mr. Edwards, I understand that as well. However, I was thinking of taking senior year music class at Fairfield in a little different direction this semester." Elise was amused but saddened. She had seen the likes of Ryan Edwards before—a cocky arrogance and smugness that said, "it's all about me, look how great I am." She knew what he was all about just in their brief interactions of a few short minutes. She had his number and realized how self-impressed and self-focused he was.

There was also a sense of delight for her in seeing the unflappable Ryan Edwards a bit off balance. "I hope you will embrace the adjustment or should I say audible. I will see you then tomorrow morning, at 7:00 a.m. sharp."

Elise Matthews then picked up her things and exited with a determined pace and ease.

CHAPTER 4

THURSDAY

**"If you can change your mind, you can change your life."
William James**

At 7:00 a.m. the following morning, Elise Matthews was waiting for Ryan Edwards to arrive. At 7:05 a.m. there was still no sign of the promising new piano student. By 7:08, Ryan sauntered into the room with a beguiling smile. He said, "Good morning, Miss Matthews." Perturbed but patient, Elise looked at her watch and asked, "Mr. Edwards, would you ever think of showing up to football practice eight minutes late?"

Ryan quickly replied, "Well, of course not. That's football."

Elise smiled patiently. She was going to set the tone early and clearly, saying, "Mr. Edwards, unfortunately, that was the kind of response I thought you were going to provide me. From now on you will be on time. And to ensure that, I now have an additional assignment for you to reinforce the point."

Ryan Edwards grinned from cheek to cheek. He couldn't wait to hear what was coming next. Poor Elise Matthews, thought Ryan, she was in for a very long and exhausting year if she thought she had any influence in changing the direction of the music department. She was going to have a very disappointing and frustrating semester if she thought she was going to direct him or influence him in any way. "Miss Matthews," Ryan replied. "And what would that possibly be?"

Elise Matthews moved over from her desk and leaning against the desk's edge continued, "You see, Mr. Edwards, I believe music, classical music, has much to teach about life itself. In fact, I believe that music can inspire one in his moral and character development. Why classical music could even make you a better football player."

Ryan Edwards recoiled. Elise Matthews stood her ground. She was not the least bit intimidated by Ryan. In fact, she was in charge now.

Elise continued, "So since you were eight minutes late, Mr. Edwards, I have an idea for you and for your behavioral and character growth. Perhaps it will translate to the football field as well. You certainly could use the help."

Ryan Edwards was stunned. Ryan had just played a terrible game over Labor Day weekend. She had just slammed him like no one had ever dared before. None of his coaches would say that when he played poorly. He was the star.

She redirected Ryan back to her assignment. "So I would like you to attend eight sessions, should we say eight extra make-up sessions for being late to 'piano practice,' starting this Sunday morning at 7:00 a.m.—one session for each minute late. Think of these sessions as your football sprints you might run if you were late to practice—which you would never do. Furthermore, I expect you will never be late again. Think of these meetings as a little extra fundamental work you might need when you blow a game, maybe because you just didn't show up on a given game day."

Ryan looked white as a ghost. Nobody ever spoke to this superstar like that, not even the principal. For the first time in his life Ryan Edwards was speechless. The air was still. The silence was painful.

Elise Matthews broke what seemed an eternal silence, "And let's see, as a final assignment, I would like you to compose a 'Playbook.' Yes, a Playbook, say eight plays, one for each minute late. Let's call them the eight values, the eight virtues, or maybe the eight 'football skills' of life— one for each day of the week plus an eighth day—that will most enhance your winning record on and off the football field—in the classroom, in service to the community, with friends, or in life generally."

She paused, waiting for him to catch up. Ryan eyed her sleek figure in a solid black dress with attraction and anger at the same time. He was horrified that he would have to do anything of substance in music class. Elise smiled in a mocking sort of way and started anew, "Now you don't have to complete this assignment until the end of the term. However, in your case, I am going to begin 'coaching' you, so to speak, starting this Sunday. I wouldn't want you to fall behind in any way."

Who was this woman, he thought. He had never known anyone like her. She was competent, attractive, and strong all at the same time. Elise added, "I would be happy to provide you suggestions for these eight virtues or values or shall we call them 'plays.' We can develop them as a team—you and me together." With a smile, she added, "So why don't we end for today. As for piano itself, here is your music book. Please read the first ten pages and be prepared to name the notes on the piano and to play the C major scale with both hands. If you have any questions, feel free to call me. Otherwise, Mr. Edwards, I will see you Sunday morning at 7:00 a.m."

Ryan then asked boldly and mockingly, "But this assignment is not a school requirement, Miss Matthews. And it's not mandatory for the music course, is it?"

Elise Matthews then replied, "You were late, Mr. Edwards. And I truly get the picture that you don't think the rules apply for you. If you are not seeking a passing grade for a course required toward graduation, then no—no it is not a mandatory assignment—if graduation is not important to you."

With that Elise Matthews picked up her things and walked out of Room 101. Ryan Edwards sat alone, lost in his shock, for what seemed an eternity.

CHAPTER 5

Saturday afternoon game

> "The journey is better than the inn."
> **Miguel de Cervantes**

It was Saturday afternoon at the Fairfield High football game. It was a close contest. Midway through the fourth quarter, the score was all tied up, 17-17. Fairfield had the ball, and Ryan Edwards was leading his team downfield with three consecutive first downs. Ryan was feeling more than confident now. He felt invincible and cocky. He knew in his mind that he had the game in hand. Ryan was losing focus on the mission of scoring a touchdown, distracted by his own self-promotion and self-aggrandizement. He was lost inside his head and his self-adulation—a sloppy aspect in his nature that more than occasionally surfaced in his behavior.

On the next play, Ryan made a bad calculation. He threw a soft, blooper pass over the middle without any pace to his wide receiver and friend, Robbie. Robbie didn't have a chance to catch it. The safety saw the scenario unfold and darted to the middle, easily picking off Ryan's pass and heading to the sidelines and sixty yards for a touchdown.

The crowd was stunned at Ryan's mistake. The opposing team fans went wild in the stands. The underdog Midtown High Cougars were given slim odds of having a chance to win the game against the all-star quarterback Ryan Edwards. It was a devastating loss for Fairfield.

Ryan was crushed after the game. He couldn't understand how it happened. It wasn't supposed to happen. In his mind, things were always supposed to go his way. Ryan Edwards was entitled and arrogant. It wasn't his fault, he told himself, so he turned to deflection. Robbie just didn't meet the ball aggressively enough. It was Robbie's fault. And Ryan let everyone know it after the game by blaming Robbie.

Ryan Edwards, in his world, was perfect. He had to be perfect or else he would crumble in his own image. His only defenses were blame and denial. He rationalized himself to safety once again in his own mind. For the moment, he was again OK with himself in his eyes. Ryan was not the problem; Robbie was.

CHAPTER 6

SUNDAY—HUMILITY:
IT IS ABOUT PERSPECTIVE AND ACCEPTANCE

> "Have more than thou showest, speak less than thou knowest."
>
> **Shakespeare**

On Sunday morning at 6:55, Ryan Edwards was sitting in his seat in Room 101. Alone with his thoughts, he began to envision how he would get out of this stranglehold with Elise Matthews. His weekend had been ruined, he played poorly in yesterday's losing game, and Saturday night was cut short for this meeting. He was disgusted with himself for failing in the game, though he could not articulate that to himself. Ryan never knew what he was feeling. He always denied acknowledging his feelings out of fear and sheer terror. He couldn't tolerate feeling anything inside.

Just then, Elise Matthews entered Room 101. "Good morning, Mr. Edwards. Sorry to hear about the game yesterday." With some disappointment, she continued, "So the team is 0-2 this season?"

Ryan was about to respond and quickly stopped himself. He wouldn't talk back to his football coach, so he restrained himself and didn't take the bait from Elise Matthews. Also, Ryan was beginning to question who was tougher—Mr. Thompson, the varsity football coach, or Miss Matthews. He was afraid to answer that question.

Elise opened saying, "So let's get started. Day 1, Sunday, any thoughts on your first virtue, your first value, Mr. Edwards?"

Ryan sadly responded, "I don't know what you are talking about." Ryan was in pain, humiliating pain, from being held captive. He felt depressed.

"Oh, come now, Mr. Edwards," Elise replied. "Don't you know what a value is, what a virtue is, what a belief is?" Elise Matthews was dressed to the nines. She wore a tight pair of jeans accentuating her terrific figure, matched with a white cotton blouse, and open-toe sandals elevated with one-inch heels. A thin black leather belt pulled it all together. Elise's shoulder length dirty blond hair was pulled back in a ponytail. Ryan thought she could pass for a very seductive twenty-one years, not thirty-one. Gathering himself, Ryan answered, "Yes."

"Well, then, tell me," Elise shot back.

Ryan added, "It is a trait or behavior."

Condescendingly Elise smiled. "Very good, Mr. Edwards. Anything else?"

"No," Ryan shot back, "that's it."

Ryan was feeling tortured. This humiliation felt far worse than any hit he had sustained on the football field. He started to sweat thinking about the ridicule he was sure to receive this afternoon from his friends and teammates. That would be unbearable, he thought. Here he was, Sunday morning, in class with Elise Matthews. The only consolation in his mind was that Elise Matthews was the hottest woman on campus. Maybe it wasn't so bad. He began again to daydream in more of his depressive thinking.

Elise Matthews wouldn't let up. "Very good, I would only add that virtuous traits tend to be positive in nature. Of course I know you have all the answers to everything; however, this one may be new to you." She took pleasure in challenging him for a short spell to get his attention and break his arrogant ways. Surely he could handle it. He was a tough guy, the toughest guy on campus. "Well, how exciting."

"I don't care, Miss Matthews," was Ryan's hopeless and helpless response.

Elise Matthews was on a quest and just warming up. "Mr. Edwards, do you know who Aristotle is?"

"I have heard of him," a defiant Ryan snapped back.

Elise Matthews took that as an opening. "Aristotle believed that moral behavior is the mean between two extremes of excess and deficiency, or the golden mean. For instance, courage, as a virtue, falls between timid behavior and reckless behavior. Courage is the golden mean or average. For instance, you might have wished for a courageous throw, not a reckless or timid one, in yesterday's game. Does this make sense?"

Ryan was stung. This was an uncommon feeling for him, if he ever felt anything at all. Normally, Ryan Edwards was in control of all situations. This was new territory for him. He was on the defense instead of on the attack. "Terrific, Miss Edwards."

Continuing Elise Matthews asked, "And do you know who Ben Franklin is?"

Ryan painfully replied, "Yes."

Pressing further she asked, "Did you know that in 1726 he developed at the age of twenty his own personal playbook, or system, to develop his character and live a virtuous life?"

Feeling even more defeated, Ryan said, "No, I didn't, Miss Matthews."

"Well then, tonight why don't you peruse this copy of his autobiography in your free time," Elise Edwards tossed a copy of Ben Franklin's autobiography on Ryan's desk. "Put together Aristotle's golden mean and Ben Franklin's character-building system, and you might learn something."

Ryan Edwards was beside himself in disbelief that he had to listen to this.

She added, "Franklin identified thirteen virtues of character which he valued. He studied and practiced them, rotating a new one each week, for a total of thirteen weeks, repeating the cycle four times a year. He also developed a score sheet and rated his performance for that particular virtue at the end of each day. Would you like to review Ben Franklin's thirteen virtues he selected? They are quite impressive. Temperance. Silence. Order. Resolution. Frugality. Industry. Sincerity. Justice. Moderation. Cleanliness. Tranquility. Chastity. Humility." Elise Matthews recited them from memory.

Almost breaking down, Ryan desperately pleaded with her, "Miss Matthews, you can't do this." Ryan felt threatened, embarrassed, and humiliated all at the same time—but by a woman—not a real coach. It was the nerve of her.

Playfully, she inquired back, "Can't do what, Mr. Edwards?"

"You can't keep me here demanding that I show up each day at 7:00 a.m.," Ryan asserted.

Exhaling, Elise responded firmly, "Mr. Edwards, you were late. But you are correct. I can't make you do any of these things. You are free to leave right now. It is your choice. If passing music class, which is a graduation requirement, is not important to you, I respect that. You're free to choose."

Ryan was losing in every way. Elise paused and let Ryan catch up. "These values can apply to life itself. They have the ability to access one's character and integrity in a similar fashion that playing classical music can access one's heart and soul."

Elise was watching to see if Ryan was tracking. "Because without a sense of values and virtues, one is without a compass in life—without the tools that lead to the development of one's character and integrity. Similarly, I also believe that without a sense for music, through performance, one is also without the ability to feel and experience life to its fullest. So Mozart, Corelli, Pachelbel, Vivaldi, Beethoven, Bach, Rameau—can be fundamental to your development of both heart and soul."

Elise Matthews understood Ryan Edwards. She admired Ryan Edwards and at the same time felt deeply sad for him. Elise Matthews knew his kind. She only had to look in the mirror to see Ryan Edwards at any moment she chose. Ryan was cocky and arrogant. He thought he was better than everyone else. His good looks carried him a long way coupled with his winning personality.

Yet it was all just a cover. Ryan Edwards always felt unsure about himself behind his screen. He believed he was never good enough—for himself or for anyone else. He was in constant, desperate pain of trying to prove himself to anyone and everyone, demonstrating evidence necessary to prove himself to himself.

Ryan could not articulate this inner discomfort. He was incapable of identifying to himself any feeling he felt; he only noticed a troubling sensation that periodically consumed his body from head to toe. It was a queasy feeling of doubt and insecurity—it was an undiscovered insecurity he had about himself. Whatever he did, however well he performed, it was not good enough. Never was it good enough.

He always found a way to reject himself, minimize his accomplishments, and torture himself in self-doubt or self-downing. Ryan believed at his deepest core that he needed to be perfect all the time in order to accept himself. Ryan was never good enough for himself, no matter how many accomplishments he recorded. So Ryan constantly grandstanded for approval, attention, assurance, admiration, and affirmation—all to feel OK about himself and to not feel alone.

But how could that be? Ryan Edwards, for all outward appearances, had the wind at his back at all times. Everything always went his way as far as an outside observer could see. But inside, there was a constant unrest and anxiety beneath the surface that plagued Ryan's every waking moment. Yes, Elise Matthews knew Ryan Edwards better than he knew himself. Every time Elise looked at him, she saw her own image; for Elise, it was like looking in the mirror. Elise Matthews once lived the same "never good enough" nightmare inside her own prison of her own construction.

Surrendering, Ryan finally said, "Fine."

Elise knew she was wearing down the unconquerable and impenetrable Ryan Edwards. "Would you like to start and describe the one virtue that perhaps is most meaningful in your life?" Elise could perceive there were layers and layers of walls between other people and the heroic Ryan Edwards. No one could get past the moat and the gates to the castle inside Ryan himself—inside his thoughts, his feelings, his dreams, his doubts, his struggles, his fears, and his hopes.

Ryan gasped, "I haven't got a clue."

Elise grew stronger, "Well, then let me suggest one for you. Since it is Sunday, let's start with the value of humility. Yes, humility will be for Sunday. Humility Sunday is your first play in your 'Playbook.'"

Humiliated, Ryan cried out, "Humility?"

Elise pushed on. "Yes, Mr. Edwards, what is humility?"

He lashed out, "I have no idea. This is bullsh . . ." Ryan caught himself and his anger before he finished his thought. Ryan was well mannered. He knew not to swear in front of women.

Growing up in a relatively affluent family, the last of four children, Ryan Edwards was the abandoned one. No one paid attention to Ryan, nor did they have any time for him. He was essentially invisible in his family; he grew up as the invisible man.

So, competitive as he was, Ryan Edwards came up with his own solution. He strove for attention and to be noticed in everything he did—sports, friends, school, you name it. Everything was to become a performance for attention, approval, admiration, and recognition. Most every encounter of his was a trial in which he had to perform and to be recognized, believing that he would ultimately be judged, good or bad, by others.

Ryan had taught himself to abdicate his self-esteem to the conditional approval of others each and every moment. Absolutely everything and every situation was a personal performance test of some sort. If he had any idea of the life-trap he had set for himself, each minute of each day, he would have fallen down in despair and emotional exhaustion. But Ryan was always strong, never the one to show his emotions. Feelings were for the weak and the frail.

"Mr. Edwards, now I'm all ears," Elise Matthews mimicked his insulting manner he had shown to her.

Ryan had learned that he had to compete in order to be noticed. But it was not something that he could explain to himself. It just happened. He set goals, and he achieved. Ryan performed all with the objective of avoiding his deep loneliness and sense of abandonment from a cold, unfeeling, but proper family. If Ryan could ever allow himself to feel anything, he might say he was sad. But that would never do to admit that something wasn't right, wasn't perfect, wasn't under control.

Ryan Edwards came from "the perfect family" where pretense and form carried the day. Substance and relationships were crowded out by a world full of singularly purposed achievements. Accomplishment was all that mattered. Relationships were a means to an end. In fact, achievement was all that mattered in Ryan's cold, emotionless family life.

Still waiting, Elise smiled a bit impatiently, "Well then, why don't we start right now. Let's try this approach to loosen you up a little bit. Name two words that describe humility and why."

Elise Matthews was going to make a point that Ryan Edwards was not in charge, as he believed he was in all aspects of his life. It was going to be a Socratic session with nothing but questions and answers, moving from one question and one thought to another, with the hope of uncovering something new for Ryan about himself. It might uncover something about how he viewed himself and how he approached life, all the while schooling him and his arrogance at the same time.

"Name a word to describe humility?" Ryan grunted back in utter disgust.

Why was Elise Matthews tormenting Ryan like this? She could have just let him slide. What made her want to make a point to him? Was it that she hated the young man she saw in front of her like she was looking in the mirror? Was it that she saw herself in him and was disgusted and ashamed with herself? She didn't quite know why she was so possessed to teach him a lesson.

Ryan continued, speaking softly but firmly, "I don't know what you are talking about." He added, "Humility is for the weak, for losers. Winners are not humble. Otherwise they would become losers. Humility is a dangerous trap to be avoided at all costs."

Elise brightened up, and she took advantage of Ryan's opening. "Great start. You're unsure, aren't you? That must feel new? You are absolutely sure that humility is a soft trait. Can I help you here, Mr. Edwards? Otherwise, we could be here all day."

With a puzzled smile, quickly thinking how he could get out of this nightmare, Ryan responded, "I am listening, Miss Matthews. Let me take some notes, if you don't mind." Ryan was sarcastic and bitter; he was beginning to feel a little beaten. This was all unfamiliar territory for him, not being in charge, and he didn't like it.

Elise was not going to let this spin out of control. She disciplined him on the spot. "Mr. Edwards, I wonder if you will be as smug in fifteen minutes as you are right now. You just may find that humility is quite courageous and strong when you're all done," pausing and looking directly at him.

"Mr. Edwards, consider that humility is first about perspective. Perspective appears in terms of your perception of yourself, of your abilities, and of your fit in the world. And to gain an honest perspective grounded in reality takes patience and awareness. Patience, Mr. Edwards, as in being patient in the fourth quarter of yesterday's game, when you threw that boneheaded pass over the middle for an interception that cost your team the game."

Ryan Edwards was aghast; he turned white. The color did not go well with his 6'1" frame, his khaki pants, sneakers, and white T-shirt. Ryan Edwards was graced with the total look of a pro athlete who is comfortable signing autographs.

"Perspective, a patient perspective," Elise continued, "to understand 'what is' right now. It's to realize what you are capable of and not capable of, to let things develop, to let things happen and run their course, to not force things on your schedule, to accept that some things just need time to develop no matter how badly you want them to happen right away. Humility requires a patient perspective with yourself and with others and your teammates.

"Humility is about a perspective that you're OK as you are right now, that things are OK right now, that others are OK right now. Are you with me, Mr. Edwards?"

In stunned disbelief, Ryan Edwards acknowledged, "Yes, Miss Matthews, I am." Ryan was absolutely speechless. She just crushed him for his error-prone play during yesterday's game. This hurt worse that Coach Thompson's words yesterday. But she had also struck a chord inside Ryan. He didn't like what he was feeling. He couldn't identify or articulate what he was feeling because Ryan never felt anything. He always stuffed feelings and emotions and moods down from where they came from anytime they arose. It was fear. He was afraid of his feelings and afraid to feel. It was threatening to his entire image of himself.

Who was she, this Elise Matthews? He was attracted to her and repulsed by her at the same time. He felt conflicted and didn't know why. Somehow Elise Matthews had just hit a few emotional nerves that he did not realize existed until now.

Growing stronger Elise Matthews barreled on, "Perspective applies not only to football, but to life as well—with your friends during the day, with yourself when you are learning a difficult new physics concept, with your parents when they give you unsolicited feedback on how to do one thing or another, with your music teacher on an early Sunday morning, with life itself when it just isn't going your way as fast as you would like it to.

Elise

"It means a perspective of patience, at age eighteen or age eighty, to acknowledge each moment as it comes, for what it is. It takes work to develop this skill of patient perspective with yourself, with others, with your circumstances—in each moment."

"Yes, Miss Matthews. You have my attention now," he replied. Ryan was captivated. She sounded incredibly cheesy with her dripping description that befit a sixty-five-year-old professor, rather than a thirty-one-year-old, 5'7", 115 pound, hot blond. But somehow she was also making sense. He seemed to feel that Elise was right somehow. Yet he was defiant and defensive too and wouldn't admit it to himself.

Elise continued, "Humility is about perspective, a perspective of understanding that there is always someone or something bigger than you. Perhaps it's God or someone or something more capable than even you, Mr. Edwards. It may be a Higher Power who is bigger and stronger and kinder and gentler—who may have just created you, given you all of your gifts and talents, and who may just call more of the shots for you in your life than you would ever imagine. That's perspective."

Ryan was getting nervous. This was now a sermon. Elise Matthews was Catholic. He thought he could have been at Mass himself. Yet at some level, he was captivated by every word that she spoke.

"Miss Matthews, you said humility is about two things," he interrupted to speed it along.

She continued, "Yes, I did. Second, humility is about acceptance, acceptance of things as they are, not as you want them to be. And that starts with yourself."

Elise was looking at Ryan with some fear as she continued—fear of a disclosure she was about to make, "This can be very hard to do. It's hard for me to do. It means cutting yourself some slack when you throw a game losing interception in front of everyone you know.

"I have learned that until you can humbly give yourself the gift of your own forgiveness, you may not be able to forgive others very easily." Elise paused for a minute to let it sink in for Ryan.

He looked puzzled. This was a new paradigm for him.

"Questions, Mr. Edwards?" she asked.

"No, Miss Matthews, not now anyway," he thoughtfully responded.

Elise picked up where she had left off, "When you are able to forgive yourself for being you and for your mistakes, you may then be able to forgive others when they mess up because they are human too.

"And you are giving them one of the most valuable gifts imaginable. You allow the other person to move on—encouraging and reassuring him that he is OK, that it is OK. It is a priceless gift one gives to another—the gift of mercy."

More mesmerized than before, Ryan Edwards simply acknowledged, "Miss Matthews, it is all so nice and theoretical. But no one does that. And if someone screws up, then they should pay the price. That's football, that's the real world." Ryan continued to fight and resist her.

Ryan was now scared. It was as if she knew exactly what was going on in his mind. How could that be, how could she know? What was it about Elise Matthews that allowed her to see inside the closed and locked walls of his heart, his mind, and his soul? He never let anyone in, ever. He blocked off all access to himself, to his feelings, to his thoughts. He kept people at a distance through surface talk and through brilliant performances on and off the field. But somehow she just seemed to know him. It was frightening and a mystery to him.

Elise Matthews smiled in response. "Mr. Edwards, you have a rough-and-tumble view of the real world. I hope that 'take no prisoners' approach doesn't take you down too far someday when things turn against you." Elise Matthews felt sorry for him for the first time.

Elise felt wounded too. His answer was exactly the answer she would have given twelve years ago. That's all she had then; that's all she naively knew. Elise regained command. "So humility, after perspective, is about acceptance, acceptance that you are not perfect, that you may be quite good at some things, but that you are also full of flaws and weaknesses in other areas, that you are just plain human, inside and out. There are always others above you and always others below you. You are not alone, and you cannot go it alone.

"In the grand scheme of things, you are a part of a larger story, though an important enough piece even when you are not the starring role. You are only a piece of the game, that even though you are the quarterback and get most of the attention, you are still only one of eleven players, and that you would be nothing without the others, that you would be toast without your line, that without your receivers who catch your errant passes and make you look good, you wouldn't be that much at all on the field."

Ryan was stung; he felt she hit him below the belt with that shot about "errant passes." Somehow it hurt more from her than it would have from others, "That hurt, Miss Matthews."

"I'm glad you noticed," she replied, knowing that he did not understand the meaning of her response. She knew that Ryan Edwards was virtually incapable of identifying, let alone acknowledging, how he was feeling at any particular moment. That's because Ryan used every defensive coping tactic possible of rationalization, denial, blame, avoidance, minimization, performance, distraction, problem solving, alcohol—you name it—to avoid feeling anything he might be feeling—fear, sadness, anger, or joy.

Elise Matthews knew because she too was frightened of her feelings while growing up. Like Ryan, she used every possible coping mechanism to duck feeling anything at all. And in doing so, Elise Matthews refused to let other people into her life and kept everyone at a distance. Elise Matthews was Ryan Edwards. That's why she knew Ryan Edwards better than he knew himself.

Now she transitioned away from football, "Off the field it is the same. Mr. Edwards, you can't go it alone either. It is the understanding that without your friends or your family or your teachers—except maybe your music teacher—or your coaches or anyone who touches your life, you wouldn't be who you are. Simply because you cannot do it all on your own, as much as you do try."

Ryan froze again. "How do you know that I run solo and do everything myself and don't ask for help."

"Because Mr. Edwards," Elise paused and then slowly revealed in a gulp, "you and I are very much alike. Mr. Edwards, we are very, very much alike. We both like to run solo."

He merely nodded, silently and gravely this time. What did she mean by that, that he and Elise Matthews were very much alike and liked to run solo? The sting was wearing off from all of her insults. He had received far worse on the football field and in the locker room. He looked up and just stared at her. "OK, Miss Matthews," he replied.

Somehow Ryan began to feel a trust with Elise Matthews at the same time. Was Elise Matthews on his side and really just trying to help him? He couldn't put his finger on it. The emotional stress of considering these things was overwhelming and intolerable for Ryan. So he put up his walls again. No one was going to get back inside now. The emotional gates were closed once more.

Elise

Elise was on a roll. "With perspective and acceptance, humility may give you a sense of gratitude in recognition of all your given gifts and talents—your good health, good looks and great ability. These traits and abilities were given to you and could just as easily have been given to someone else. You might just realize, with some humility, that you are more lucky and fortunate than you are good, even though you have worked hard to develop what you have.

"Gratitude is humble acceptance in action.

"In spite of all your pursuits to prove your worth through approval, Mr. Edwards, you might just come to see that you are already 'there' and don't have to strive desperately toward some unidentifiable, intangible, unknowable achievement goal in order to prove to yourself and to others that you are OK. Perhaps, you are OK right now as you are."

Ryan sat motionless—stunned, frozen, perhaps even in awe but not grasping why he felt as he did. Ryan arrogantly and defensively fired back, "Really, Miss Matthews. You don't say."

Ryan was scared that Elise Matthews might be right. Yet he only knew that at an indescribable and visceral level equivalent to being sick to one's stomach. There was no possible way Ryan Edwards had the ability for this awareness nor have the personal insight to know what was going on inside him. He was frightened.

Elise Matthews wasn't going to be pushed around by the self-proclaimed pretty boy. "Mr. Edwards, I am not sure if you are buying what I have just said. If you want another opinion, read the *Book of Job*."

Ryan inquired back, "And what would I learn there, Miss Matthews." He was angry, hurt, threatened, frustrated, and afraid, but he did not know that.

"Job regained his attitude of humility and trust in God but only because of his experience of suffering. And by the look on your face, I'd say you have suffered enough. Humility is developed but only at a price, the price of honesty, grounded in reality, and an acceptance of that reality—by surrendering and letting go. Well, Mr. Edwards, I think that is enough for today." Elise was tired of his arrogance. She playfully concluded. "I want to say I truly enjoyed this dialogue and discussion with you this morning. I am looking forward to continuing tomorrow morning at 7:00 a.m. sharp. Would it help you if I shared tomorrow's virtuous value?"

"Yes, Miss Edwards, it would," Ryan responded with sarcasm.

"But first," she asked, "Mr. Edwards, to finish for today, how would you describe humility in two words."

Exasperated, Ryan paused and said, "Humility is about perspective and acceptance." He wasn't sure how he even uttered that response. Somehow it seemed to work.

Elise Matthews glowed in shock and surprise. "Mr. Edwards, yes. If you learn nothing else about humility remember two things.

"One, remember, perspective—that there is always someone above you and below you, that you are better off than some, worse off than others, that everyone, and I mean everyone, will have their defining challenges and that no one can go it all alone.

"Two, remember, acceptance—accepting things as they are and not as we want them to be and demand them to be. It's accepting yourself as you are right now by recognizing the good and bad within you, the strong and weak in you, the elegant and flawed in you, so that you can be on your own side in good times and in bad times. You may come to accept yourself as you are in order to accept others and accept life as they are, ultimately knowing that you will be able to handle whatever challenges come your way."

Ryan Edwards was paralyzed in every way. He couldn't think, he couldn't feel, and he couldn't move. What did she mean that by the look on his face, he had suffered enough? Could she possibly see behind his screens and masks, his self-centered fears, his self-doubts, his independent self-sufficiency, and his mask of pride? Elise Matthews wrapped it up. "Very well. If Sunday is about humility, Monday is about discipline. Enjoy the rest of your weekend, Mr. Edwards. I do want to say though, that in spite of that final interception yesterday, I think you played very well, and you lead the team decisively. They do seem to want to follow you, in spite of yourself."

Elise Matthews left Room 101. As the door swung shut, Ryan Edwards was left alone in the dark, left with his own thoughts—many, many troubling thoughts.

CHAPTER 7

Monday—Discipline: It is about Visualization and Practice

> "The most pathetic person in the world is someone who has sight, but has no vision."
>
> Helen Keller

Monday morning, 6:55 a.m., Ryan Edwards was settled in his seat in Room 101. Miss Matthews arrived shortly thereafter. With no hesitation, she began the session with a burst of energy. "Mr. Edwards, tell me about discipline. What does it mean to you?"

Ryan felt depressed and dejected. It was only 7:05 a.m. in the morning. "Miss Matthews, I don't know."

Elise Matthews shot back, "A little disappointing, Mr. Edwards, but very well. It's only Monday.

"First, think of discipline as visualization. You know what that is?"

"Yes, Miss Matthews," Ryan replied. "I do it all the time in football. I visualize a game a week in advance, imagining how it is going to turn out. I visualize certain scenarios and situations and how I will deal with them if they arise in the upcoming game. It helps a lot."

Elise was pleased to see she had finally made some connection with Ryan Edwards. "Good, Mr. Edwards. Visualization helps you focus for self-control. Self-control can mean thought control, emotional control, physical control, and spiritual control.

"Thought control is managing your thoughts, emotional control is managing your feelings, physical control is managing your actions, and spiritual control is managing your beliefs. Discipline, through visualization, can help you focus in all four areas, each day, minute by minute. Following, Mr. Edwards?"

Ryan was following her thread. "Yes, Miss Matthews, I am."

"Take controlling your thoughts. You can control your thoughts in the moment with pictures—yes, control your thoughts through picture destinations of where you want to be. Get on the right side of your brain and visualize where you want to be. Pick a destination and create a vivid picture. Start there. It can silence the sometimes rapid, high volume noise inside your head."

Ryan softened. "This is the first thing that makes sense." Ryan Edwards was all about control—control of every situation and outcome in his life. It's what gave him comfort, a perceived feeling of being in control. "I visualize what I want to see happen on the football field," Ryan added.

Visualization was a strong point for Ryan Edwards. It was a way to lift himself and his team up when they were behind in a game. With an image of what he wanted to see happen, he could help lead the team to execute. Visualization was the foundation for several of his fourth quarter comeback wins.

What Ryan did not understand was that to be in control, sometimes the humility of letting go was necessary. Sometimes accepting that you cannot control everything you'd like and expect in life can free you. Not resisting what is, not fighting what is, and letting go to what is can actually make you stronger.

Encouraged, Elise Matthews continued, "As visualization can help control your thoughts, visualization can also help control your feelings, your actions, and your beliefs. Mr. Edwards, do you think you manage, in the moment, how you think, what you feel, how you act, what you believe? This kind of awareness can become a daily routine, at age eighteen or eighty, just by being present in the moment. You have choice to be present and aware in each moment.

"How you think about things, Mr. Edwards, can start a domino chain—from what you think, to how you feel, to what you do. Your thoughts can shape what you believe and what you value. You have choices—thinking, feeling, doing, believing choices."

Ryan was both amused and puzzled, "A little out there, don't you think, Miss Matthews?"

"Visualization helps you define your purpose and goals." Undeterred by his insolence, Elise proceeded, "Goals motivate you to act and get started. Without goals and their deadlines—for the day, the week, the year or the next five years—you can get stuck, unable to move forward. Does that ever happen to you Mr. Edwards?"

Ryan was busted, "Yes, it does, Miss Matthews. It does. I get stuck sometimes."

"Goals provide you purpose and meaning. They help you answer the question 'Where am I going?'

Elise

"Be aware of your goals, of your purpose, of where you are going. Visualize your picture destinations to help define your purpose and your passion.

"You are your own photographer, Mr. Edwards, taking pictures and snapshots of your life as you want to see it unfold.

"Visualization of your goals, by getting on the right side of your brain, will help you stop the endless chatter up inside your head."

Elise Matthews suffered from OCD. Her mind was constantly in motion, thinking things, and rethinking the same things, again and again. She couldn't easily turn off her brain from obsessively replaying and ruminating the same thoughts, good and bad, over and over again. Like a truck stuck in the mud, hopelessly spinning its wheels, Elise's mind could go into overdrive too. She could make any matter worse simply by applying more pressure on the cognitive accelerator in her head.

Ryan held an expressionless face. He wondered how Elise Matthews knew that he often had endless, merciless chatter and conversation, usually negative and catastrophic, going on inside his head? She knew the way his mind and his brain worked better than he did.

Ryan Edwards lived up inside his head, struggling constantly to turn off his obsessive thinking. Ryan had no idea he had this challenge. He lived with a constant undercurrent of ongoing thoughts about his doubts, fears, and worries, constantly playing in his head like background music. His thoughts were telling him that he might fail, or that he isn't good enough—unless he succeeded at that "next thing." The problem was that there was always another "next thing" required to prove to himself that he was good enough.

"Second, think of discipline as practice," Elise Matthews broke the silence.

"You practice daily to achieve the goals or visualized destinations you have pictured on the right side of your brain. Practice. Practice. Practice. Do you know who John Wooden is?"

"Yes, Miss Matthews," Ryan chuckled. "I do. But this one should be interesting." Ryan Edwards was wondering what a music teacher could know about John Wooden, The Wizard of Westwood, and perhaps the greatest college basketball coach ever.

Elise Matthews explained without reacting to Ryan's insolence. "When asked upon retiring if he missed the coaching, the championships, the attention, the trophies, John Wooden simply said, 'I miss the practices.'"

Ryan Edwards could not resist. "No, Miss Matthews, I didn't know that. And I am fascinated that I might be learning this fact from a music teacher."

Elise Matthews smiled coolly. "Careful, Mr. Edwards. Don't assume that because my passion is now music, that I am ignorant of sports and all its life lessons. You don't even know whether I might have played the sport myself, do you?"

Ryan Edwards's color changed to pale white. Was Elise Matthews a jock too? What couldn't she do, what didn't she have going for her? Ryan regained his composure in an adolescent way to respond to her question. "No, Miss Matthews, and I don't really care. But please continue." Ryan Edwards was angry. He felt outmatched by Elise Matthews, but he couldn't figure out why.

Ryan Edwards did not know that Elise Matthews was an exceptional athlete at a prestigious New England College, lettering in three sports—field hockey, basketball, and lacrosse—and captain of two of the teams. Additionally, Elise Matthews killed it in the classroom with a 3.8 GPA. She was the femme fatale of her college. Soon Ryan would come to learn these things about Elise Matthews and wonder

Elise

how such a stunning woman in her early thirties would be all alone, teaching high school music. She too "downed herself" growing up in high school, in spite of all of her extraordinary accomplishments.

"In time you might just care, Mr. Edwards." Elise Matthews responded gently, "The greatest satisfaction in life for John Wooden was not the games, not the wins, not the eleven championship trophies. It was the practices. It was the daily, uncelebrated, not so exciting, practices. John Wooden believed life was more about the practice and the preparation than it was about the games and the wins.

"Discipline is also about practice—how you practice, your daily routines—to carry out the vision of your picture destination you've created in your mind."

Ryan was spellbound. Who was this music teacher? She knew things she shouldn't know because she was only a dumb piano teacher. He thought he had heard it all. Yet she surprised him again. Who was Elise Matthews? She was getting stronger all the time. She somehow knew what she was talking about—something Ryan never imagined possible from her on this athletic topic. Ryan Edwards was back on his heels—an uncharacteristic position for him.

Frustrated with Ryan, Elise caught herself with awareness and compassion. She had been in his shoes years ago. Elise knew that he wasn't as tough as he proclaimed to be. Ryan was like a turtle—hard exterior, soft interior—just like herself.

She continued, "Practice requires daily repetition. You persevere and endure in whatever your goal or passion is. And you do so through persistent and daily repetition, building your skills, your confidence and your dignity."

It was almost 7:30 a.m. Looking at the clock, Elise pressed on, "Practice requires resiliency, getting up when you are knocked down.

Resiliency is the ability to restart yourself in a positive way when things don't go your way. Churchill said, 'Success is the ability to go from failure to failure without losing your enthusiasm.'"

Ryan was spellbound. "Churchill, Miss Matthews?" Ryan countered again, "Miss Matthews, what makes you so sure of yourself. You keep telling me how it is. You seem to have all the answers," appearing more confident, indignant, and smug with each second.

Elise remained composed. "I have my opinions, I have my views, Mr. Edwards, but not the answers. I only know what works for me through my hard fought experiences. I don't know what will work for you. I have the answers for me. It is for you to choose the right answers for you."

Elise thought for a moment and took a risk. "And I do believe as I have said before, Mr. Edwards, that you and I are similar in many ways."

Ryan couldn't resist the follow-up. "And how might we be similar, Miss Matthews?"

Elise Matthews paused for a moment to set up her final blow of the session. "We are both quite arrogant because we have all the ability," she replied. Ryan Edwards was completely off balance. She nailed him, and herself, with her honesty. Reality was all new territory for Ryan in his perfect, illusory world of fantasy that he had constructed. Ryan Edwards was a legend in his own mind in order to protect his fragile self-esteem. Elise was earning Ryan's respect as well as his contempt.

Nothing was going to slow her down now. "Start with a goal and a visual picture, Mr. Edwards. Purpose will motivate you to act. Motivation will instill the discipline to begin, to focus, to persevere, to recover, and to begin again.

Elise summarized discipline in two words.

Elise

"Discipline is, one, about visualization—of a goal or aspiration. It's getting over to the right side of your brain with purpose and passion, freeing you from your obsessive thinking up inside your head. Visualization keeps you focused on your goal. It helps you forget yourself and live in the real world.

"Second, discipline is about practice. Practice is performing routines to accomplish your goal. Your picture goal refuels you as you persevere through the drudgery of repetitive practice. The visual destination sustains you through difficulties, setbacks, and disappointments. It can help you trust that things will be OK and that you will get through the challenge you face.

"Visualize then practice. Visualize then practice."

Ryan asked with some curiosity. "So why, Miss Matthews, why is Monday about discipline?"

Elise Matthews exhaled. "Because Monday is the toughest day of the week. It is the day of getting started, at school, at home, at work. Do you really like Monday mornings, Mr. Edwards? I can't say that I do. I must admit that Mondays are tough for me. Getting started, getting restarted, turning on my own 'action ignition' is difficult sometimes. But the discipline of creating picture destinations of where I want to go often gets me started."

Having some fun, Ryan tried to trip Elise again. "And why is Sunday about humility?"

She knew what he was doing but did not take the bait. "Sunday is a day of thanks and gratitude for the blessings given to us. Humility is about thanks for those blessings. Gratitude can bring peace—when humility is genuine." She was solemn in her tone.

"OK, Miss Matthews," he responded in a somber voice. Ryan still resisted much of what Elise had shared over the first two sessions. She had made him feel uncomfortable. Who was Elise Matthews?

Elise Matthews refocused the discussion. "Mr. Edwards, in two words, what does discipline mean to you?"

Ryan deflected her question. "No, Miss Matthews, please you do the honors, I went yesterday."

"Mr. Edwards, I just gave you the answer, if you were listening," Elise accepted without irritation, "Discipline is about visualization and practice."

Elise had an idea. "There is another way to remember the eight values. This is, after all, music class. Why don't we also think of these values as notes on the scale? How about the scale of C major, since that is the first scale you learned the other day? That's the simplest and cleanest scale of them all. So start with middle C, middle C is for humility, or humility Sunday. Then go to the D note, D is for discipline, or discipline Monday.

That way, Mr. Edwards, every time you play the scale of C, you can be reminded of the eight values."

"Yes, Miss Edwards," he said with reluctant respect.

Elise concluded, "Tuesday, Mr. Edwards, will be about faith."

"Faith? I can hardly wait," Ryan chuckled with impertinence.

Patiently and almost motherly, Elise said, "Yes. Mr. Edwards, why don't you see if you can bring something to the table on this one." With that Elise Matthews stood up and walked out of Room 101, again leaving Ryan Edwards with something to think about.

CHAPTER 8

TUESDAY—FAITH: IT IS ABOUT BELIEF AND TRUST

> "A weak faith is weakened by predicaments and catastrophes, whereas a strong faith is strengthened by them."
>
> Victor Frankl

Tuesday morning, 6:55 a.m., Ryan Edwards was back in his seat. He now had the routine down. What was a major annoyance now became an intriguing show. What could Miss Matthews come up with next on the topic of faith? Elise entered Room 101 at precisely 6:59 a.m.

Elise greeted Ryan as she entered, "Good morning, Mr. Edwards. Thanks for being on time. Let's get right to it. We don't have that much time for a topic such as this. Any thoughts you would like to share about faith?"

Ryan quickly responded, "Not really, Miss Matthews."

Elise Matthews was disappointed. She berated him, "And why is that, Mr. Edwards?"

He quickly responded, "I'm not much for religion."

Elise held her ground. "Mr. Edwards, this is becoming predictable. I won't allow you to do this all week. Wednesday, you will lead."

She walked around the front of her desk, directly facing Ryan. With disappointment for his insubordination, she said, "Faith isn't just about religion. Faith is more about spirituality than religion alone."

Elise Matthews could see this session was going to be a struggle. "For me, faith is first about belief. A belief is something that you accept as true. You are what you believe.

"If you believed, Mr. Edwards, that your quarterback days were coming to an end, you might view this season and this year's practices a little bit differently than if you believed that your best quarterback days lay ahead of you in college and beyond. Is that a fair statement?"

Ryan was stunned. How could she know his innermost thoughts and feelings? It was a discussion he had with himself in his mind over and over again. Ryan didn't know his own feelings. Feeling exposed, Ryan responded sheepishly, "Well, yes, Miss Matthews, I might approach it differently."

Elise ignored his retort. "It may be important for you, Mr. Edwards, to understand what it is that you accept as true, what you believe is true, implicitly and explicitly, deep down inside yourself. Your beliefs will drive your thoughts, your feelings, and your behaviors.

"Your beliefs are your strongest thoughts, and you probably have no conscious idea what your deepest beliefs are about yourself and about the world around you. You may be totally unaware of what you believe about yourself to yourself. That's your self-talk."

Elise looked into Ryan's eyes. "First, try to see faith as your beliefs—your self-beliefs, your beliefs about others, your beliefs about how the world works, and your religious or spiritual beliefs. Your beliefs influence your self-identity, your passions, your values, your purpose, your plans, and your goals."

Now she was going to give him a little test. "For instance, Mr. Edwards, do you believe in honesty? Is honesty something you value? If so, then you might resist the opportunity and act with integrity and character when presented with the opportunity to cheat on a test, even knowing that you could get away with it. Why might that be?"

Ryan retreated, off balance with the question. "Because it's not the right thing to do?"

Elise smiled. "Yes. If you believe in honesty, you would walk away. If you did not value honesty, you might just take the bait and cheat."

Elise continued, "Similarly, Mr. Edwards, if you believe in yourself, you will perform better than if you doubt yourself—every time, every situation, on and off the field.

"We all believe in ourselves sometimes, and we all doubt ourselves too. We usually are unaware of it at the time and in the moment. You might feel and do better, if you were more aware of what you say to yourself—when you down yourself by not being on your own side or when you encourage yourself with positive self-talk and affirmations.

Ryan Edwards was mesmerized. He couldn't believe this was happening. He was learning a few things that would help his game on the field.

Elise Matthews was finding her stride. "You can believe in anything you choose to believe in. You can believe in honesty, cheating, loyalty, or hard work as examples. You can believe in your competence or incompetence, your worthiness or unworthiness.

"The single most important thing about your beliefs is that you choose them for yourself. Know what they are for you. Know what you believe explicitly. Your beliefs define you more than you realize."

Ryan stopped her in frustration, "I don't need to spend time thinking about what I believe. I have confidence in what I can do. It's simple, Miss Matthews. You're complicating it, starting with humility, then discipline, and now faith. And you're wasting my time." Why was Ryan defensive all of a sudden? Did he not believe in himself? He wasn't so sure.

Elise knew that she would have responded as Ryan did when she was his age. Elise behaved like Ryan when she was on the top of her game twelve years ago. But then things didn't go so well. For a series of reasons, things in Elise Matthews's world began to unravel. The invincible and arrogant Elise Matthews got knocked down. She went from being on top of her game to becoming overcome with paralyzing self-doubt.

Elise Matthews became depressed because she didn't measure up to her own exceedingly high standards and impossible personal achievement expectations after some crushing setbacks. She didn't cut herself any slack. She crucified herself for failing. She acted out in a retreating and avoidant fashion. She went through a stage of underage drinking and alcohol abuse to soften the emotional pain and pressure she inflicted upon herself. Because of her impossible expectations, she masked herself in grandiosity. She had set herself up for her own fall by age fifteen. It was only a matter of time before she fell.

"Mr. Edwards, I agree with you, when things are going your way. But what happens when they don't? What do you do when you fail? What if things don't always work out? Where do you go when you fall?"

"I don't fail. I never have. I always come through." Ryan was indignant. He didn't really buy what he was saying right now. He felt threatened by her question, with the notion that he could possibly fail. Ryan felt sick, exposed with doubt for the first time in his life. He felt naked and found out.

She tried not to attack back. She knew all too well this person who was responding. Yes, it was Ryan Edwards, but it was also Elise Matthews, who was speaking right now.

"Well, Mr. Edwards, for those of us who aren't perfect, who are mere mortals, who make mistakes, who fail now and again, beliefs can be a refuge when you're wounded. Your beliefs about yourself can heal you, sustain you, and help repair you when you're down. Or, if they are self-downing and distorted beliefs, they can tear you apart even further."

He was shaken. Elise Matthews was scaring the fearless Ryan Edwards. He resisted with denial and deflection. "Aren't you being a little negative, Miss Matthews? Where's your positive mental attitude?" He was being a jerk.

Unflappably, Elise Matthews pressed on without acknowledging his insolence. "Your beliefs can help you succeed in achievement and recover from failure.

"Your beliefs help shape your thoughts, your feelings, and your actions—for your overall happiness in life. Your beliefs influence your thoughts, which influence your feelings, which drive your actions."

Ryan Edwards sat motionless. He had never thought about the impact of his beliefs on his life. It made intuitive sense. He hated to admit it, but he was now intrigued. Further he hated to admit that Elise Matthews could be right.

"Two, faith is about trust." Elise Matthews became stronger, "It means committing to your beliefs of what is true. You don't question, you don't rationalize, you don't analyze. You merely trust your beliefs once you have chosen them. And you stay true to your beliefs in difficult and challenging times.

"You let go to your beliefs and surrender to your beliefs through trust—trust in yourself, trust in your teammates, trust in your receivers to catch the ball, trust in your offensive line to save your hide from getting sacked, trust in your friends to be loyal and supportive, trust in God. You merely trust in what you believe. Trust allows you to act without hesitation."

Ryan was annoyed at that last shot about getting sacked, but he restrained himself. He was stung by her comment. But why did he care about what she thought, he wondered.

"Mr. Edwards, by knowing and trusting your beliefs, you can surrender yourself to the outcomes in your life you desperately want to control but cannot. It means letting go to your beliefs—which is counterintuitive. It is the opposite of what a hard charger like you, or I, would ever think to do. This is very easy to talk about, but very difficult to do in practice."

Elise asked Ryan a question, "Do you believe in God, Mr. Edwards?"

"I do, Miss Matthews. I look in the mirror, and oftentimes I see God." Ryan was over the line with cockiness, but it only reflected his insecurity. He was feeling sick inside. He didn't know why he said what he just did. He began to sweat. Ryan Edwards never sweat about anything.

She ignored his immaturity. "Well, I do. And it is my belief that God is on my side. I believe that all I need to do is what's the right thing for me. After I have done all that I can possibly do in a situation, I try to let go and let God take over. It's hard for me to do. It requires faith and trust in my belief in God—that things will work out OK when I'm faced with a challenge.

Elise

"I believe and trust that I'm not alone and that someone or something bigger than myself is always there with me, in good times and in bad times. My belief in God helps me trust that I am not alone and can handle whatever challenge life serves me. I can surrender and sometimes let go. But it's hard to do all the time."

Ryan Edwards was shocked again. "I know what I believe, Miss Matthews. I have faith and trust in myself."

Elise finished her thought, "Honestly, Mr. Edwards? Well, I am not very good at trusting myself or at trusting others. I try to control everything in my life—out of lack of trust—even though I intellectually know that I should let go. It's hard for me to let go. It takes faith to surrender and let go. It takes courage to let go."

Ryan softened his stance, "When things get tough, I try harder and redouble my efforts until I get it done." He was afraid of how she would respond to his comment. Elise Matthews intimidated Ryan Edwards.

She seemed pleased. "Mr. Edwards, have you ever considered that when you find yourself in the dark it may require a different mindset? Consider that as things get worse, you may need to loosen your grip on things and soften your hold on life in order to cope with your challenge? Having a vise grip when things don't turn out your way is natural. But it doesn't seem to work out very well when you press too hard—in anything."

Elise knew she had his attention at this point. "Loosening your grip by letting go is a counterintuitive move. It's having a relaxed tension in whatever you are doing in life. You work hard, you try to work through it. But you loosen your grip by trusting that you will get through the situation, letting go to God when you have done all you can do.

"It's about abandoning yourself in a trusting fashion that things will work out and that you will get through the situation. It's simple to talk about but very difficult to do."

Ryan Edwards felt deluged just about now. This exercise was no longer as simple as he had thought. He was intuitive enough to realize that Elise Matthews seemed to know what she was talking about. This he understood.

Elise Matthews regained her focus. "Faith, or belief and trust, can create a willingness to surrender and let go to someone else or to something greater than you." Ryan was mentally exhausted, and it was only 7:25 a.m.

"Faith is knowing, Mr. Edwards. Doubt is wondering," Elise concluded. "Well, I see we are out of time. Same time tomorrow, Mr. Edwards."

Finishing off the lesson Elise Matthews closed, "Oh, and Mr. Edwards, faith in two words is about belief and trust. Will that work for you, I presume? Tuesday, faith, is about belief and trust. And faith is the E note, the third note, in the key of C major.

Ryan was dazed, and he blurted out, "Yes, Miss Matthews. And tomorrow is about?"

Smiling, Elise Matthews responded slowly, "Let's see. Wednesday, Wednesday is about courage, the value of courage. I expect your participation."

"And let me ask you one more question, Mr. Edwards, in preparation for tomorrow—are you willing and able to ask for help when you are in trouble? Do you have the courage to ask for help? Let's continue this tomorrow." Elise Matthews walked out. Ryan Edwards was alone one more time in Room 101.

CHAPTER 9

PIANO PRACTICE—SESSION 1

"I don't mind what happens."
Jiddu Krishnamurti

Ryan Edwards was now in an unfamiliar zone. He was doubtful he could handle the piano work required. He found his way over to the music center, and went into a practice room. After sitting down at the piano, Ryan stared at the keyboard. He didn't know where to start or what to do. He tried to read the C major scale notes on the workbook page that Elise Matthews handed out, but he just could not follow it very well. He was completely lost.

After staring at the piano sheet for ten minutes, Ryan gathered himself and tried to play again. Still he found no success as he banged away on the keys. He was dejected, an uncommon feeling for Ryan. Maybe there was something to the idea of asking for help and not going it alone all the time as Elise Matthews suggested. He quickly dismissed that crazy and fleeting thought. It was wrong, he knew, to show weakness or ask for help.

Ryan stopped, picked up his music sheets, and left the practice room. On the way out he passed by Julie, another senior classmate. Julie was really cute, but not in Ryan's mind. Julie was not part of the "A team" socially. He labeled her awkward, though nice enough.

Ryan hung with only the "cool kids" and the attractive crowd. He was judgmental. Ryan's girlfriend, Kate, was the head cheerleader with knockout looks. All the guys said she was the best-looking girl in the school. Ryan was proud that Kate was his girlfriend. She showed well, and she kept up the image and pretense Ryan so desperately wanted and needed to maintain.

But if Ryan had ever stopped to think about it, he would have concluded that Kate was not that nice. In fact, she was a bitch when she chose to be. Life was all on her terms and only in regard to herself. But Ryan never went there. He was satisfied enough that he had the prettiest girl in school as his girlfriend, regardless of how she treated everyone else, including him.

That might be because Ryan could not see that he could be mean to his friends as well—just the male version. Ryan Edwards had a blind spot for Kate, minimizing her abusive behavior. To call it out would mean he would have to admit that he could be a jerk himself. So he stuck with his denial strategy.

Julie noticed Ryan as she was walking toward the music center. He was approaching her as he exited. "Hi, Ryan," Julie said with enthusiasm. She had a personality that was positively contagious and that always brought people up. It was one of her gifts she shared generously with others. Maybe that was the real definition of being "hot."

Ryan looked at her briefly and quickly responded, "Hi," without acknowledging Julie by name. As he passed by Julie, he wondered why she was always so happy? She was not even that cute, he had always told himself, compared to Kate. But there was something awfully attractive about Julie at the same time. Ryan was confused, because she looked cute and attractive just then. How could that be? But Ryan had to get to football practice, so he dismissed his momentary anxiety that perhaps he didn't have it all figured out.

CHAPTER 10

WEDNESDAY—COURAGE: IT IS ABOUT CHOICE AND CHANGE

"The greatest test of courage is to bear defeat without losing heart."

Robert Ingersoll

Like clockwork, Ryan Edwards was again punctual at 6:55 a.m. and sitting in his seat. Elise Matthews walked into the room soon afterward. Talking while walking, she quickly began, "Good morning, Mr. Edwards." A no-nonsense manner directed Elise. "Let's get started. Tell me about courage."

"Courage is action," Ryan responded with an air of confidence and self-admiration. He was looking for her approval but could not see that himself.

Elise Matthews, startled, encouraged Ryan, "Mr. Edwards, continue. Yes, courage is in part about action."

Ryan knew about courage and toughness as a superstar athlete in multiple sports. "There is no courage without action. You've got to keep moving. Paralysis is fear and discouragement, or the opposite of courage. You must keep moving, whether you are winning or losing. To stop is to die."

For the first time, Elise Matthews was impressed. In fact she was learning something herself. "Very good, Mr. Edwards. Courage is about action. But what is it that fuels action?"

Ryan thought for quite awhile but had no answer.

Elise helped Ryan out. "Courage to act is fueled by choice.

"Courage is first about choice." Elise made direct eye contact with Ryan. "Choice is about asking the question, 'Is that the right thing to do?'"

She paused to see if Ryan was following her, "It's asking that question explicitly and deciding explicitly based on your values.

"Then courage is responding appropriately in one of three forms—think, feel, do. You are free to choose—what to think, how to feel, what to do—anytime, anywhere, in any situation."

"I don't understand," Ryan was both puzzled and curious.

Elise Matthews proceeded patiently, "Three ways to choose, Mr. Edwards—thinking, feeling, doing. Let's start with thinking.

"First, courage is a thinking choice. Are you thinking the right thoughts? Are you choosing to think positive or negative thoughts in your self-talk to yourself? Are you up or down, advancing or retreating, are you thinking the right way, in big or little challenges?

"How you think is everything. Thought control is self-control. It takes enormous courage to control your thoughts, particularly under adversity. 'Think To Cope.' It's hard to do."

Ryan was following every word Elise Matthews spoke. "Yes, Miss Matthews."

Elise continued, "You know quite a bit about courage as you have demonstrated in your famous fourth-quarter-comeback wins. It's your focused optimistic thinking, thinking positive thoughts that you chose to think during the game. We are free to choose how we think, positively or negatively, each and every moment. We just aren't aware this fact."

Ryan liked what he was hearing. He wondered now if he was in a philosophy class two thousand five hundred years ago tutored by one of the greats—Heraclitus, Socrates, Plato, Aristotle, or Epictetus. Was Ryan Edwards beginning to like Elise Matthews? She was growing on him in a beguiling way. "Miss Matthews, how do you know all this? You're just a piano teacher."

Elise Matthews smiled in amusement at the insulting label Ryan just slapped on her. "The second way to choose, Mr. Edwards?

"Second, courage is a feeling choice. Are you feeling up? Are you allowing yourself to feel down? Are you aware of what you are feeling? Do you have the courage to feel your emotions? Do you choose to feel, to acknowledge and to embrace your emotions? Or do you choose to reject them, stuff them, avoid them, and escape from them? Do you have the courage to feel anything at all?

"The feeling choice is the translation of your thoughts into emotions. Are you feeling happy or sad, up or down, winning or losing? Can you even identify what you are feeling? Do you even know how you feel right now?

"Your feelings are a direct result of how think. How you think determines how you feel.

"Your feelings follow your thinking. Change your thinking and you change your feeling.

"It takes courage to identify, acknowledge, and accept how you feel in the moment. It's easy to deny or stuff your painful feeling saying, 'I'm fine. It's nothing.' You are free to choose how you feel each moment. We just aren't aware of that fact either."

Ryan felt he was just doused with a fire hose of wisdom water. "I don't feel much of anything. I just do. I think, I solve, and I do."

Elise liked that Ryan was engaged—for once. "Mr. Edwards, that may be true, however, action is often preceded by feeling. Attitudes are feeling thoughts, which come from your thinking. Your thoughts are strongly influenced by your core beliefs about yourself, your beliefs about others, and your beliefs about how the world works—more strongly than you'd ever imagine." Elise checked Ryan with a glance to see if he was still keeping up with her.

"The third way to choose, Mr. Edwards?

"Third, courage is a doing choice. Along with, side by side, and after thinking and feeling comes doing. Courage is a doing choice about consistent habits of action. Your thoughts lead to your feelings, your feelings color your doings—all three are choices you make.

"Think to feel, feel to do, 'think-feel-do'—it's a graceful waltz. You have three choices you can make each moment. You need all three steps together to dance in life. It's the ultimate triangle offense to live and to cope with life as it comes to you."

Ryan resisted mockingly, "Triangle offense? Wow. I don't dance. It's all too mechanical, Miss Matthews. And I'm a guy who is all about the mechanics and the fundamentals."

Elise Matthews patiently let Ryan finish rambling so that she could proceed. "The three ways—thinking, feeling, doing—work together influencing each other. You can think your way into feeling. You can think your way into doing. You can do your way into thinking. You can do your way into feeling. You can feel your way into thinking. You can feel your way into doing. All three ways—think, feel, do—reinforce one another in a graceful rhythm.

"Start anywhere, and move in any direction. Think-feel-do. It can be your dance of life. It can be your triangle offense in life."

"It's a little too cute, Miss Matthews," Ryan challenged, though tentatively and unconvincingly. He wasn't sure of himself. He was desperately afraid that she might be right—again. This was becoming all too threatening for him.

Elise Matthews proposed a scenario, "After Saturday's game, Mr. Edwards, weren't you down? Didn't you go out and practice on your own. Didn't you feel better afterward? Didn't you believe once again that you would recover? Didn't you again believe that you would win your next game? Didn't you talk your way into feeling? Didn't you think your way into doing? Didn't you then act? And through your action, your restart, and your renewed practice effort, didn't you begin to feel better about yourself, your situation, and your next game? Didn't you do your way into thinking and feeling better? Didn't you recover through your think-feel-do routine and regain hope—based on your action, based on your improved thinking? Didn't your feelings then improve?

"I believe you just may have thought and acted your way into feeling better—to get 'unstuck' which may have just improved your mood. You can think and do your way into feeling better. Your thoughts and actions can affect your feelings.

"Imagine that your feelings are your emotional thermostat. They may tell you about your thinking and doing, like a thermostat tells you what the temperature is. Feelings are your thinking thermostat; emotions are your doing thermostat.

"See the cycle as self-renewing and self-reinforcing. With some awareness, you can feel your way into monitoring your thinking and doing. With some reflection, you can think your way into doing. With some positive thinking, you can do your way into feeling better. It's a triangle—a triangle offense—think-feel-do."

Ryan Edwards reflected in astonishment, "Yes, I did." He was stunned. Could she be right on this too?

Elise became Socratic once again. "So courage is first about choice. Choose, Mr. Edwards, choose. Choose your thoughts, choose your feelings, and choose your actions.

"Also choose your beliefs—about yourself, about others, about the world.

"Choose your attitude each moment, choose your outlook each moment, choose your disposition in response to any situation.

"Choose to win the next five minutes with a positive attitude—five minutes at a time.

"What else is courage?"

"I don't know," he responded.

"What is the purpose of courage?" Elise challenged him.

"Action? Growth? Change? I don't know." He tried his best.

"Yes, Mr. Edwards, change. Second, courage is about change. Courage is the willingness and the ability to change."

Elise Matthews was smiling inside. "Courage is all about change. Do you have the ability, and perhaps more importantly, the willingness to change?

"Do you want to change? Do you want to improve in some way? Do you want to grow? Do you want to contribute, help others, or heal yourself?

"Or are you resistant to change? Do you use the standard tools of denial, minimization, and justification?

"Change is threatening, risky and uncertain. Willingness is not always easy. Readiness is not always easy. Staying the same feels safe and secure—that's avoidance."

The bell was going to ring. Elise added, "So courage, courage in two words—is about choice and change.

"Choice is the 'think-feel-do' choice. Everything you think and feel and do is based on choices you make. You choose your thoughts if you are aware enough to do so. Those thoughts influence how you choose to feel. Those feelings influence what you choose to do, and how you do it."

"Change is the willingness and the ability to try—to try again and to try then again with motivation toward a purpose."

Elise completed her thought. "The change question is 'do I want to get better, in some way, wherever I am right now?' It's your choice to decide for change and growth.

"Courage—or choice and change—can be hard. That is why you see so many failed New Year's resolutions. To choose, to decide, can be difficult. Napoleon said, 'Nothing is more difficult, and therefore more precious, than to be able to decide.' Change is threatening and unfamiliar. But the courage to change can also be exciting. Growth is possible, if you are willing and able to try, if you have a willing and able attitude and disposition, if you are game."

Not forgetting to tie these lessons to music theory, Elise concluded, "So in the key of C major, courage—or choice and change—represent the F note."

Ryan Edwards hung on every word Elise Matthews spoke. It was trance-like. Elise concluded the session. "Thursday is about optimism." With that proclamation, she briskly left Room 101.

"Yes, Miss Matthews." Ryan was catching her enthusiasm almost like one catches a cold. He was feeling now that he was the student, and Elise Matthews was the teacher, and even more so the coach. Never would Ryan have ever entertained this notion. Something was changing. Ryan Edwards was changing.

Was he starting to respect Elise Matthews? Was she his advocate and not his enemy? Was he feeling now that Elise Matthews was somehow looking out for him, rather than trying to crucify him? He wondered why. He sensed in his stomach that Elise Matthews perhaps liked him, almost as if she somehow picked him out as a pet project of hers.

Ryan Edwards left Room 101 but with an uneasiness and indefinable distress. Whatever was happening, it was out of his control. That sensation alone threatened Ryan Edwards deeply.

CHAPTER 11

Thursday—Optimism: It is about Attitude and Hope

"For myself I am an optimist - it does not seem to be much use being anything else."

             Winston Churchill

Thursday morning, 6:55 a.m., Ryan Edwards was in his seat, bizarrely looking forward to the next thirty minutes. Never in his high school academic career had he been genuinely interested in anything—other than football. A sneaking suspicion hit him that perhaps he had met his match, that his loud, high-anxiety coaches were puppy dogs compared to what he was subjected to currently, albeit most civilly, and seductively from Elise Matthews, his music teacher.

Ryan Edwards respectfully stood up and said, "Good morning, Miss Matthews." Ryan went bright red with embarrassment. He rarely stood up for anyone, even though he always knew it was the right thing to do. He was well mannered. But Ryan was always cocky enough to believe that the rules didn't apply to him, that he had a different set of rules. So he had no idea why he stood up. Perhaps it was out of a new respect? Ryan Edwards was not in control, the one thing he always insisted on in any situation.

Elise Matthews returned a kind greeting. "Good Morning, Ryan," she said in a moment of vulnerable discomfort. But she caught herself calling Ryan by his first name and quickly recovered, replacing the distance and space she required through her formality. "Mr. Edwards, what can you tell me about optimism?"

He had clearly thought this one through overnight. "Optimism is about positive attitude."

She was impressed, "Nice start, Mr. Edwards.

"Optimism is first about attitude."

Ryan began to explain, "Attitude is how you look at a situation, will you succeed or will you fail, in advance of the outcome."

Elise was reassuring but with a spice of harmless sarcasm. "I'm most impressed. You will be quite a musician in time."

Ryan was wounded by her slight. Initially he restrained himself.

Ryan Edwards was a tough guy and the star quarterback. Everyone knew that about Ryan. But what everyone didn't know was that Ryan Edwards had severe emotional sunburns. Ryan Edwards was incredibly sensitive to any form of criticism. He developed these sunburns and emotional injuries from his childhood and in part from a lifetime of crucifying himself for never being good enough, no matter how well he performed.

And Ryan Edwards was a performer. So given the hand he had dealt himself, he had no choice. His destination was always perfection and always to be better than everyone else.

Life was nothing but a competition and a comparison contest with others in order to prove to himself that he was OK, each and every day.

There was no margin for error, no tolerance for human error in Ryan's life. He had constructed a game for himself in which he would never win. Ryan regained himself and was still not sure if Elise was just innocently playing with him or criticizing him.

Ryan hated criticism and evaluation and judgment of any kind. That's because it was all he ever did to himself, each and every moment—judge, and evaluate and criticize and find fault in everything he himself did. Nothing was ever good enough. It was never OK, and he was never OK.

Unknowingly, he was on a performance treadmill desperately trying to escape the self-imposed prison of rules, beliefs, ideas, truths, absolutes and notions he had constructed for himself.

In spite of his ongoing accomplishments that everyone else admired—everyone else but himself—Ryan could not accept himself. Ryan was his own worst enemy, and he didn't even realize it.

Ryan Edwards didn't have a chance in this game, on this playing field, by these rules. He would always lose because of how he defined the rules of his game of life. It was a painful, sad and unnecessary tragedy. Ryan wasn't thinking about being human at all. He was in search of perfection.

The sting of Elise Matthews's last comment sent his mind racing. Ryan finally lashed out, feeling rejected and angry, "Miss Matthews, this has nothing to do with music."

Watching his reactions, Elise was both amused and saddened. She knew what went on in his own self-talk, chalk talk, translation session. "Ah, but it does, Mr. Edwards, remember the key of C major. The C note is for humility. The D note is for discipline. The E note is for faith. The F note is for courage. And the G note now is for Optimism. Now please, Mr. Edwards, continue. If optimism is about attitude, what else is it about?"

Ryan was now deflated and out of bullets for the day on the topic of optimism. "What else is there?"

Elise took over. "As you stated, optimism is about attitude, which creates enthusiasm for something specific. Enthusiasm is fuel. The fuel of enthusiasm leads to hope.

"Optimism is second about hope."

He agreed defensively, "Fine." Elise Matthews had struck a few chords and nerves inside Ryan Edwards that he did not want revealed. They were too threatening to admit. He was also becoming enthusiastic about something else . . . Elise Matthews—was he becoming attracted to Elise Matthews?

"And what about your attitude toward yourself?" Elise continued. "Is your self-attitude one of optimism or pessimism, confidence or doubt, acceptance or rejection, self-esteeming or self-loathing?"

Elise paused to give Ryan a minute to process what she was offering. "Hope, then, is about the future—about realizing the picture destination in your mind.

"Optimism is about hope.

"Hope is what you feel when you are looking forward to something with expectation and a positive attitude. Thomas Monson said, 'Hope is putting faith to work when doubting would be much easier.' Hope is an essential emotional fuel."

Ryan was now wondering . . . no, he knew that Elise Matthews somehow played sports. But she was just a music teacher. How? "Yes, Miss Matthews," he affirmed while he was still off in his own thoughts about her.

Ryan looked at the clock, which Elise noticed. "We'll finish early this morning, Mr. Edwards. Yes, I think we're done for today. Friday is about kindness. See you tomorrow." She quickly began to exit the room.

Elise Matthews was changing too through this process. There were seeds of an attachment growing inside her. She was unsettled, which she always felt was unbecoming. Was she becoming attracted to Ryan Edwards in an odd, empathic but innocent way? What did she see in him—a mirror image of herself?

Recognizing her sloppy attentiveness and daydreaming, Elise Matthews quickly caught herself and stopped. "Mr. Edwards, in two words, what is optimism?"

Ryan Edwards looked up with a knowing smile. "How about attitude and hope." He took his time now. "Optimism is about attitude and hope—a positive attitude right now and a hopeful outlook for the future."

She was speechless. "Yes, Mr. Edwards, yes. And optimism is the fifth note in the key of C major. Optimism is the G note." Still off balance, Elise Matthews once again exited Room 101.

CHAPTER 12

PIANO PRACTICE—SESSION 2

"When I do good, I feel good; when I do bad, I feel bad, and that is my religion."

                                                    Abraham Lincoln

That Thursday afternoon, Ryan went back to the music center. He had a little time before football practice. He found an empty piano room and sat himself down on the piano bench. He pulled out his sheet music and tried to play the C scale with his right hand. It was painful to watch. He had no fingering skills. Instead of playing C-D-E with his thumb, index, and middle fingers, he simply pecked, note by note, with his second finger. At least he was able to find middle C as a starting point.

Oddly, Ryan Edwards was thinking about the first five values as he was working with the C major scale. C-D-E-F-G. Humility-Discipline-Faith-Courage-Optimism. He shuddered in disgust to think that he was actually using Elise Matthews's memory technique.

At that moment, Julie was coming out of an adjacent piano room. The piano sonata she just played was by Mozart. She played it exquisitely. Noticing Ryan in his practice room, she stepped in to say hi. "Hello, Ryan."

Ryan turned and caught Julie's eyes. They were beautiful blue eyes. Of course Ryan had no idea before this moment what color they were, nor did he notice that he had noticed her eyes. But he did feel struck by something in Julie. But that was as far as it went. "Hi, Julie," Ryan responded somewhat dejectedly.

Julie felt an uncomfortable silence and tried to make some small talk. "How's it going?"

Ryan exhaled. "Not so well. I can't play this C scale." Ryan repeated what he had just done moments before. Was Ryan asking for help? Did he admit he was struggling? Why?

Julie looked on with a cute and a forgiving smile, the one a mother might have for her three-year-old boy trying to learn something new. Julie then came into the room. Without thought or any uncomfortable feeling, Julie sat down next to Ryan on the piano bench.

It was Ryan, however, who now felt uncomfortable. He was out of his element. And she sat right next to him touching up to his side but without any sense of embarrassment or social self-consciousness. She merely was there to help.

"Ryan," she said, "Try this." Julie then proceeded to play the C major scale effortlessly. She played C-D-E—thumb, index finger, and middle finger. She continued F-G-A-B-C—thumb under, index finger, middle finger, fourth finger, and fifth finger. She then repeated it going up and down three octaves, three times. She then reached her left hand across Ryan's stomach, touching him, and proceeded to play the C scale with both hands up and down three octaves. She could do this in her sleep. She had spent hours playing the Hanon exercise book of piano drills. She knew them all and played them beautifully. Her innocence was attractive in itself.

Julie stopped, and there was a silence. Ryan was undone. He may even have been sweating. He didn't know. With her right hand, Julie then picked up Ryan's right hand and placed it on the piano with his thumb starting at middle C. It was a touch that felt different in every way. She slowly guided Ryan through a one-octave C scale with the correct fingering technique: C, D, E—thumb, index finger, then middle finger. She guided Ryan's thumb under his middle finger to the F key: F, G, A, B, C—thumb, 2, 3, 4, 5 fingers.

Ryan was inundated emotionally. His circuits were firing on all cylinders. He was emotionally out of control. That was because Ryan had little ability for emotional control. He couldn't recognize even one of his feelings—let alone control one or embrace it or sit with it or enjoy it or feel it or accept it or appreciate it.

He did tell himself that Julie was incredibly gentle and graceful in her effortless, innocent manner. In that moment Julie was very attractive to Ryan. It surprised him. He had thought that Julie was nice enough, but now she radiated a way and a manner that was alluring. She was cute being just herself. He had never thought of her that way before. In fact, he had never thought of her at all before.

Next to his bombshell girlfriend, Kate, Julie was not nearly as externally pretty, until now. But inside, Julie was far more stunning than Kate would ever be. That's because Kate wasn't very nice. Yet Julie was the definition of nice. She found the good in everyone. That's almost all she could see. And just being oneself, how could anyone ever do that without pretense or mask or costume?

Ryan was beginning to see that maybe he wasn't that nice, that maybe he was a little selfish, too, like Kate. Julie with her kind manner made Ryan pause for the first time and wonder whether maybe he didn't have it all figured out. But maybe Julie had.

Maybe Ryan and Kate were mean and self-centered, and that Julie had just pulled the curtain back on this fact. Maybe Ryan and Kate got away with being selfish and a little nasty because they could due to their extraordinary good looks.

Ryan regained himself. "Wow, thanks, Julie."

With that, Julie stood up and walked to the door. "Ryan, try that. First with one hand, then add the left. Do it for three or four octaves. Then repeat it again and again. Let me know if you want any help after you try this for awhile." Julie looked into Ryan's eyes with a kind smile. She wasn't judging him. She was enjoying the moment.

Maybe it was because Ryan intuitively knew that Julie wasn't judging him that Ryan felt so relaxed. He knew no matter what he did, Julie would not judge him. It wasn't her way.

Maybe Julie was attractive to Ryan because she somehow made it safe for Ryan to be just himself—unfiltered without all the masks and roles and costumes.

Maybe Julie made Ryan feel for the first time in his life comfortable being just himself as he was—strengths and flaws together. How freeing it was to not feel judged.

Ryan thanked her again. "Julie, I'll do that. Thanks."

With that Julie had to leave. "Ryan, I have to get to my next class. Bye."

This time Ryan responded back, "Bye, Julie," and smiled himself, a happy smile, like he hadn't smiled in a long time, as long as he could remember. Ryan had just been struck in the heart and didn't know it.

CHAPTER 13

FRIDAY—KINDNESS:
IT IS ABOUT PATIENCE AND GENTLENESS

> "Be kind, for everyone you meet is fighting a hard battle."
> **Plato**

On Friday morning at 6:58 a.m., Ryan Edwards entered room 101. Elise Matthews was already seated at her desk.

With a confident smile he greeted her, "Good morning, Miss Matthews."

Elise did not look up from her desk. "Good morning, Mr. Edwards."

This time Ryan started it off with a petulant comment, "Kindness, Miss Edwards, why would I value that? I play football. It's about being tough and about winning. Winning is not about kindness."

Elise volleyed back, "Really, Mr. Edwards? Then what is kindness about?"

Ryan was bashful and sarcastic. "This is not my specialty. I don't know."

Elise Matthews smiled reassuringly. "Mr. Edwards, that's true. Kindness is not your specialty, especially self-kindness. You know you don't have to always be so hard on yourself. There is another way."

Elise Matthews made Ryan Edwards nervous with that last comment. He really didn't understand what she had said. The value of kindness reminded Ryan of the contrast between Julie and Kate, and between Julie and himself. Ryan was questioning if Julie had it right. Perhaps Kate and he had it wrong with their arrogant self-absorption.

Ryan now understood what Elise Matthews had said, and it wasn't all that good. So to protect himself in resistance and denial, Ryan became defensive once again. "Really, Miss Matthews? Do you think so? Not if I am going where I intend to go."

Elise hesitated for what seemed a minute and then softened in an unusual way. "I have an admission to make, Mr. Edwards. Kindness was not, and still is not, my strength either. I use a tough exterior to get through life because I am shy. I created barriers with others. I tried to do everything myself. I never asked for help. I never let anyone in. And I can tell you from painful experience that it doesn't work very well in the long run.

"In my view, you are far better off when you soften your stance, open yourself up to others, and can ask others for help now and then. Reveal something about yourself, and let other people into your world."

Ryan Edwards froze. He was shocked. Elise Matthews had just shared something acutely personal about herself. No one knew anything about her. The story on Elise Matthews was that she was beautiful, she was sexy, she was confident, she was smart, she was plain hot, but she was also fully guarded and let no one in. Nobody really knew Elise Matthews beyond her accomplishments. Nobody knew Elise Matthews's story.

"Kindness is first about patience," Elise began.

"Patience begins with yourself, or self-patience. Only then do you have the capacity and room for patience with others. Patience requires tolerating yourself and including others when you could just as easily exclude them. It's non-judgmentally accepting others' beliefs or behaviors even though they differ from yours.

"Patience works on its own time schedule, not on yours or mine." Ryan grew tense. He was busted. Ryan was anything but patient with himself. Rather he crucified himself daily, hourly, whenever he was less than perfect.

No wonder he was tough on others. He demanded perfection from himself and from others—perfection no one could possibly deliver. Was his impatience with others more about his anger with himself for being imperfect?

"Kindness is second about gentleness," Elise shared. "Can you handle a situation with gentleness—calm, assured, patient, empathetic gentleness?"

"Gentleness, Miss Matthews? Are you suggesting that I throw my passes gently next game or that the team should hit the opposing team gently?"

Elise couldn't wait for Ryan's next reaction after these words. "John Wooden said, 'There is nothing stronger than gentleness.' He learned this lesson of gentleness from his father."

Ryan Edwards was tired of her and her quotes, but he was impressed she knew them. Mockingly, he inquired, "And why do you know so much about basketball?"

Elise Matthews smiled confidently. "It will surprise you, Mr. Edwards, but I was captain of my college basketball team. And basketball wasn't even my sport."

He couldn't breathe. Ryan was floored. Elise Matthews was a jock too. He knew it. He sensed it all the while. She was a hot jock. Elise Matthews was a great athlete too. It didn't make sense before because she was just the music teacher and played the piano. Ryan was thrown off balance.

So Elise Matthews was an athlete; she always looked so fit. She was "cut" as any guy would like to be. She was in great shape. Now it all made sense. Elise Matthews was an athlete too.

She again commanded the floor. "Patience and gentleness are the essence of kindness.

"They open up opportunities for you. Attention is one—listening with attention is one of the greatest gifts you can give to another person. It's the gift of one's complete and patient attention. Attention is kindness through patient listening and gentle reassurance."

Ryan Edwards stared in silence. She had his full and complete attention.

Elise Matthews continued, "Kindness, or patience and gentleness, requires empathy."

"Empathy starts with self-empathy. Empathy is understanding who you are—good and bad, strengths and weaknesses—and tolerating who you are as you are. It's recognizing, appreciating and accepting your limitations."

"This is counterintuitive. When you accept yourself as you are, you get out of your own way. You take yourself out of the picture. You can focus on others and things other than yourself."

Elise Matthews didn't pause. "Kindness also depends on compassion. Compassion is feeling the pain of others as if it were your own pain and wanting to help alleviate that person's pain. And compassion begins with self-compassion."

Ryan was touched in a new way, feeling emotions he had never felt before. Elise Matthews had a whole other side to her, once you made it past her Fort Knox exterior. She was kind and warm and gentle, but she never let anyone see it—until now. She was always tough—never sweet, never vulnerable, never open.

She noticed Ryan's moved reaction. "Mr. Edwards, that's enough for today.

"You may not remember any of these discussions ten years from now. They won't all sink in now, if they ever have meaning at all. Like learning a sport or an instrument or any new skill—kindness takes time to develop. Work at it again and again, figuring out how it works for you."

He was in a panic and on unfamiliar ground. "I'm not sure that I will be able to do that, Miss Matthews."

Elise Matthews responded gently, "Mr. Edwards, try to have patience and gentleness with yourself for once. Relax. Take a breath. Exhale."

Ryan sheepishly retorted, "Yes, Miss Matthews." He noticed the time. Where had it gone? The thirty-minute session flew by in what seemed seconds.

Ryan took the initiative and summarized the lesson, "Miss Matthews, kindness is about patience and gentleness." Ryan Edwards desperately wanted to know.

She nodded thoughtfully, "Yes, Mr. Edwards, Friday kindness is about patience and gentleness. Kindness is the A note in the key of C major.

"And let's say that for tomorrow, Saturday is about charity."

Ryan shot back, "What? On Saturday, game day?"

Elise Matthews remained composed. "Yes, Mr. Edwards, Saturday. And I would encourage you to show up tomorrow." As the door slammed shut after her departure, Ryan was at a loss for words—a very rare and a very uncomfortable occasion.

Two things occurred to Ryan Edwards. One, Elise Matthews was now in charge, far tougher than any coach he had ever encountered. Two, Elise was building a custom plan tailored for Ryan Edwards. But this plan or Playbook now had little or nothing to do with football.

CHAPTER 14

SATURDAY—CHARITY: IT IS ABOUT SHARING AND FORGIVING

"No one is useless in this world who lightens the burden of another."
                                    Charles Dickens

It was Saturday morning, 6:55 a.m., in Room 101. Ryan Edwards was now wondering if he was going crazy. He had a game at 2:00 p.m. He should still be asleep. Why did he show up?

Elise Matthews came in. "Good morning, Mr. Edwards."

Feeling defeated, he replied, "Good morning, Miss Matthews."

Elise started her class. "I know you have a game, so let's get to it. What is charity about?"

Ryan Edwards returned the question with a vinegar tone, "What is charity?"

Elise Matthews did not take the bait. "Yes."

Ryan Edwards gave up. "Charity is—I don't know."

Elise Matthews became impatient herself now. She didn't want to be there on a Saturday morning any more than he did. She was going to make this one quick.

"Charity is first about sharing, Mr. Edwards.

"Sharing is opening yourself up to others so people can get to know who you are. It is sharing your thoughts and your feelings and yourself with others. Sharing is vulnerable territory because it takes personal and emotional risk. Sharing is standing up for yourself and asserting yourself because you believe in yourself."

He acknowledged, "I don't share my thoughts or my feelings with anyone. They are private. They are nobody's business." It now appeared more clearly than ever to Elise Matthews that like her, Ryan was also extremely vulnerable.

Ryan Edwards didn't want to expose himself in any way that might make him look weak or dumb. He was as guarded as she was, maybe even more so. It was like watching a restless caged tiger at the zoo, trying to escape, trying to get free, strong and scared at the same time. But free from what? Free from himself and his self-imposed mental notions, ideas, and plain madness? Ryan was in a cognitive prison 24-7; he lived under maximum security.

Elise gazed into Ryan's eyes. "Neither did I, Mr. Edwards, neither did I share any of my thoughts or feelings. It worked brilliantly, so I thought, until it didn't work at all." Ryan could see the pain in her face.

Elise Matthews paused for a few seconds. "And now I'm alone because of it." You could hear only silence. Ryan felt sad for her. This was new for Ryan, because he usually only thought of himself. What had happened to Elise Matthews? He wanted to know. She was hurt and had made a big mistake. Was she warning Ryan Edwards not to do the same?

"Second, charity is about forgiving." Elise proceeded back on point. "It starts with forgiving yourself for being you, with all your strengths and all your flaws, with all your brilliance and all your mistakes.

"Do you, Mr. Edwards, have the capacity to forgive yourself with empathy and compassion?"

Elise saw that Ryan was extremely uncomfortable with her last question by his horror-stricken expression. "Once you forgive yourself, you can, through charity, forgive others. It's making amends with you and with others. It's allowing others to make amends with you.

"It could be as simple, Mr. Edwards, as saying 'I'm sorry' or letting someone off the hook saying 'it's OK.' It's simple, but we seem to make it hard.

"How infrequently do we say we are sorry because we blew it? As importantly, how infrequently do we say we are sorry to ourselves because we blew it? How infrequently do we forgive someone else for making a mistake? How infrequently do we forgive ourselves when we make a mistake?

"Instead, we build up resentments with ourselves and resentments with others—for a hurt received. The hurt can be either self-initiated or externally received from someone else.

"We let it sit—for hours, for days, for weeks, for years. It just might be, Mr. Edwards, that because we can't forgive ourselves and can't accept ourselves as we are, we also can't forgive others and can't accept others as they are."

Ryan was struck by what Elise was saying, but he was also thinking of the game. "Thank you, Miss Matthews."

Elise noticed Ryan was already at the game in his mind, "Mr. Edwards, did you ever wonder why in an emergency on a plane the flight attendant instructs you to put on your own oxygen mask first? Well, maybe that's because you can't help others until you help yourself first."

Elise concluded for the day, "Mr. Edwards, you are dismissed, after you summarize what charity is in two words."

With an exhale of relief, Ryan responded, "Charity is about sharing and forgiving."

Elise concluded by saying, "Yes, Mr. Edwards, and charity is the B note in the key of C major. Come back tomorrow for the eighth and final day."

Ryan Edwards exploded in near rage. "But Miss Matthews, you said a week. I have endured enough lectures, don't you think? I have paid my price."

Elise Matthews stood her ground. "Mr. Edwards, a week—this is an eight-day week, as you were eight minutes late that first day. Remember? Eight minutes late, so eight days, so eight values, and so eight virtues. See you tomorrow. It will all make sense then. And good luck in today's game." Elise Matthews left with a swift pace.

Smug as can be Ryan Edwards shot back, "Miss Matthews, a week is seven days."

Turning back with amusement, she said, "Mr. Edwards, tell that to the Beatles."

CHAPTER 15

GAME TIME

"Character is like a tree and reputation like a shadow. The shadow is what we think of it; the tree is the real thing."

Abraham Lincoln

Ryan Edwards and Fairfield High were about to have the biggest game of their season. After a disappointing loss the week before, Fairfield was going against the division title winner of the previous year.

Although Ryan knew the pressure that lay upon his shoulders for the team and for his own expectations, he remained cool. Somehow he noticed before the start of the game how he was feeling. Normally he would speed right through that phase and feel nothing—stuffing down inside himself any feeling that might arise.

This time was different. Today he noticed what he was feeling, and he observed what he was thinking without judgment.

He just let his thoughts and his feelings flow easily and gracefully throughout his mind and within his body without evaluating them or criticizing them or interpreting them. He freely breathed in and out and just smiled at his thoughts and his feelings of fear, of hope, of determination, of doubt, of optimism, of anxiety, of worry, and of assurance.

He felt them all and he let them inside and then he let them go out again. He merely observed his feelings for what they were, embracing all of them at the same time.

During the game, Ryan was on fire. He was cool. He was confident. He was strong. Yet he was scared. He was worried. He had moments of doubt. He thought and felt all of those thoughts and feelings. He watched those thoughts and feelings pass through him without resistance during the entire game.

Ryan marched down the field on the very first drive. First down after first down, he called his own plays. He exuded a "can do" confidence that was virtually contagious to everyone of his offensive teammates. Ryan believed in himself, and therefore, they all believed in him too. Ryan had his teammates' following without exception, without doubt—with crisp, confident execution.

The first drive was an eighty-yard, eight-minute, touchdown march. Then the Fairfield defense responded in turn, picking up Ryan's emotional flu as well. The Fairfield defense stopped the title defenders on their first series, preventing a single first down.

Fairfield received the ball back, and Ryan Edwards again led the team on a sixty-yard, seven-minute, touchdown drive. The score was quickly 14-0, early in the second quarter.

And so it continued throughout the game. Fairfield dominated the title defenders the entire game. The final score was 42–14. Fairfield easily knocked off the defending champs. Ryan Edwards led the charge—cool, confident, poised, and aware of his thoughts, feelings, and action. It was clearly the best game of his still growing career.

CHAPTER 16

Everyday—Presence:
It is about Breathing and Awareness

> "If you miss the present moment, you miss your appointment with life."
>
> Thich Nhat Hanh

At 6:55 a.m. Sunday morning Ryan Edwards was seated in Room 101. It was a cold, crisp morning. The air was still, and you could feel it.

Ryan looked back on yesterday's game. He had left Elise Matthews at 7:30 a.m., later going to the locker room. He suited up, and played the game of his life. Ryan Edwards passed for three hundred yards, threw three touchdown passes, and led the team to six touchdown scores.

He looked and acted like a veteran college quarterback, with an intangible inner sense of just knowing and trusting his stuff without even trying. His sense of timing was almost warped on the field. He at no time was aware of the physical time during the afternoon. Three hours had come and gone, in retrospect seeming only like a few moments. It was any senior quarterback's dream interview. For the college scouts, and for Ryan Edwards, the performance couldn't have come at a better time in the season.

As he was heading into the locker room yesterday after the game, Ryan caught sight of Elise Matthews sitting in the stands. Making eye contact with Elise, Ryan smiled at her. Something happened on the field in the game, and Ryan had a suspicion that his instruction during the week from Elise Matthews had something to do with it.

Elise Matthews, one not to be caught off guard, was undone. His smile of thanks and gratitude was validating for Elise on that brisk September afternoon. Ryan Edwards was evolving and transforming. He was beginning to feel both uncomfortable with the changes in himself yet glad at the same time.

Interrupting Ryan's deep reflection, Elise Matthews walked into Room 101 promptly at 7:00 a.m. She was surprised to see Ryan already in his seat. He looked tired and yet eager—like a little boy. She thought it was cute and smiled, but she didn't have the heart to say that out loud and humiliate him.

Again, Ryan stood up like a gentleman. "Good morning, Miss Matthews."

Elise was nicely surprised at his simple, elegant, gentlemanly sign of respect toward her. Ryan was disarming in his gesture. If he were ten years older and not her student, Elise Matthews would have found Ryan Edwards extremely attractive, if for no other reason than that single gesture of respect alone. "Thank you, Mr. Edwards, please be seated. This is the last day of 'the week.' It's about presence. What does presence mean to you?"

Ryan responded doubtfully, "It means being here?"

Elise paused, about to cut right to the chase. But then she regained her composure and patience. "Mr. Edwards, nice start, yes it does. Tell me more."

Ryan was flustered. "It simply means being here, right now. I think I was present yesterday in the game. I may have been present for the first time—no second-guessing, no evaluating, no judging, no fearing, no criticizing, and no self-commentating—there was no filtering through my lens. I just was there—being, observing, feeling, doing, and intuiting. I lost all track of time and self-consciousness. I wonder if I will ever be able to do that again." Ryan was reflective, looking at the floor in front of his desk. It was like a confession.

Elise Matthews was moved. She reassured him gently, "Yes, Mr. Edwards, you were all of that yesterday. You'll find that it comes and it goes, again and again, throughout your football career and your life. You were certainly present during the game yesterday.

"Presence is first about breathing.

"How you breathe, consciously and mindfully, determines what you perceive. Without presence through your breath, you are unprotected in life—like having no offensive line in front of you on the football field.

Ryan was amused but listening. Breathing, really? How stupid. We all know how to breathe, Ryan thought. We do it all day long or else we wouldn't be alive. Then a sudden and terrifying epiphany struck Ryan like a powerful helmet blow to the abdomen. Perhaps we really don't know how to breathe. What if, in a sense, we are dead, or asleep? Was this where Elise Matthews was leading him? What if she were right about presence and breathing too?

Ryan again resisted, "Breathing, Miss Matthews? Really. I'm an athlete."

Elise Matthews showed a broad, slow, empathic smile. She looked terrific. Dressed in a simple, tan cotton dress, her hair pulled back, she was plain, pure and clean in her elegance with no makeup. Elise looked ten years younger with her simple beauty and calm expression. She was comfortable in her own skin and with what she was suggesting. Her face was without anxiety or doubt. She was relaxed with an appropriate tension at the same time. She was confident in knowing who she was. And she was also ready for Sunday Mass, following this morning mission enlightening Ryan Edwards.

Elise Matthews paused and said, "Mr. Edwards, yes, you are a terrific physical athlete."

Then Elise made her claim, "But an 'Emotional Athlete,' Mr. Edwards, not in the least."

Ryan was struck through the heart with that last remark. He was an athlete, but he wasn't? What on earth was an Emotional Athlete? "An Emotional Athlete, Miss Matthews? What's that? Do you have a 'Playbook' on that one too?"

Yet beneath his bravado and disrespect, he did not know why he felt found out. Aggression was Ryan's cover under stress. Despite his achievements, Ryan's entire life was driven by fear—fear of failure, fear of loss, fear of disapproval, fear of abandonment, fear of rejection. It was fear of being inferior, fear of being unworthy, fear of being inadequate. His life was fueled by fear—sometimes helpful, other times not at all.

Ryan's life was about fear and cognitive anxiety, projecting into the future, watching a scary movie. Fear was both a positive motivator for accomplishment and a negative, emotionally depressing inhibitor at the same time.

Ryan feared his emotions as much or more than anything else. Ryan made fun of guys with emotions. Emotions were for girls. Athletes are strong, cool, and in control. Guys don't have emotions, let alone share them. Emotions are for the weak. It's what he learned at home. Brains and ability and accomplishment are all that really mattered. Ryan always dismissed his emotions the instant they arose inside him. He would stuff them into his personal trash basket with great energy, force, and unknowing fear.

Ryan Edwards was afraid of his emotions and afraid to feel his feelings. Feeling his feelings may have been the greatest fear in his life. But since Ryan was asleep and unaware, he could not articulate that insight about himself to himself.

His defense and strategy against his fear was to attack back upon threat and figure the rest out later. After pausing to let Ryan sit with the blow just received, Elise continued, "Breathing requires you to both inhale and exhale.

"People like you and me get it half right. We inhale. That's what some achievers do. People like you and me hold our breath and do not exhale. We try to control everything—every event and every outcome for ourselves and for others. That's what makes us tight.

"When you breathe mindfully, inhaling and exhaling, you become more aware of yourself, of your surroundings, of others. When you breathe mindfully, in and out, you can observe yourself in the moment while doing and participating. You can accept the moment without controlling the moment.

"Presence is second about awareness.

"Awareness, Mr. Edwards, is your armor. In any situation, awareness can be your best defense. Your awareness armor can protect you and help you dance the 'think-feel-do' waltz engaging in life in a stronger way.

Elise Matthews refueled Ryan Edwards with some encouragement, "Without knowing it, Mr. Edwards, your performance yesterday was all about presence. I would bet your breathing was balanced—inhaling and exhaling—without self-critiquing or self-monitoring. This may have allowed you to be fully and intuitively aware of your thoughts, your feelings, and your actions."

Ryan was thinking as Elise spoke. He knew that he was in an indescribably positive zone during yesterday's game. He was breathing and flowing throughout the game as Elise described. "Yes, Miss Matthews, all of what you said is true. How did you know?" Did his breathing—inhaling and exhaling—help him in his game yesterday?

Elise Matthews thought to herself for a moment. Then she answered, "Mr. Edwards, you discovered it for yourself during the game. It was easy to see. Your breathing increased your awareness of the moment. You were present, and it made the difference for you."

She continued, "Yesterday you experienced the eighth and perhaps most important value—presence through breathing and awareness. Anyone can find it and experience it—with courage to try and faith to let go in the moment."

Ryan was tired and wished he were home and asleep. Childishly he tried to trap Elise Matthews, "So Miss Matthews, what's the name of this eighth day of the week."

Miss Matthews continued smiled patiently, "Mr. Edwards, the eighth day is 'Everyday,' it's for Everyday presence—it is your eighth day of the week.

"Presence is the foundation upon which all seven of the other values stand. Without presence, without being in the moment, right here, right now, you cannot experience life as fully as you might, nor can you live the other seven emotional values."

Ryan yawned in fatigue and doubt. "Miss Matthews, you're wearing me out."

Elise was undeterred. "Again, presence is about breathing and awareness. Yes, I can see you are laughing. Breathing, everyone does it and it is very easy. This must be some kind of joke. However, I would have you consider that even though you and I may take some fifty thousand breaths each day, we aren't very good at it. We take it for granted. We have bad breathing habits. We do it very poorly.

"There are two parts to breathing—inhaling and exhaling. We all seem to get the first part right—the inhale. But we just can't seem to get the second part down—the exhale. We spend most of our time and our lives holding on to our breath out of fear of one thing or another.

"It may be anxiety about an upcoming test, concern over too much school work, fear of not getting asked to the prom, fear of rejection in asking someone to the prom, fear of not getting accepted to college, fear of not getting asked back to teach a second year of music, or even fear of never finding the love of your life.

"Fear is the inhale. Worry is the inhale. Doubt is the inhale. Anxiety is the inhale.

"But faith, faith is the exhale. Belief is the exhale. Trust is the exhale. Surrender is the exhale. Letting go is the exhale. Humility is the exhale. Acceptance is the exhale. Asking for help is the exhale.

"Life is the exhale.

"Breathing is a choice too. It becomes habit. Our choices become our habits.

"We can hold on to our breath with each inhale—holding on to our fears, worries, doubts, and anxieties.

"Or we can let go of our breath with each exhale—surrendering our fears, worries, doubts, and anxieties.

"Breathing is a choice too.

"But this is only my experience. It works for me. It may not work for you.

"I resisted exhaling for years, thinking I could do it all by myself, just like you. I just inhaled. Asking for help, admitting I need other people, exhaling—that's honesty, that's humility. I was never able to exhale when I was your age. I was never able to ask for help. I was never able to let go. I was too proud. It's hard to do. It takes practice. I still don't get it right all the time. But I exhale more often than I used to."

Elise had Ryan's attention. He guessed she was speaking about herself now. What was that fear about not ever finding the love of one's life? What happened with her boyfriend, or rather ex-boyfriend? She had taken a great risk revealing herself and her personal fears. Could Elise Matthews be vulnerable too? Why share a genuine part of her to him? Why had she revealed herself to Ryan? It was risky and real. No pretense, no posturing, no masks, no costumes, no roles—it was pure honesty. She was emotionally naked.

His eight meetings with Elise were influencing Ryan. He was changing as he listened to her words. His beliefs were changing. Ryan looked at her differently. Elise Matthews was a knockout by all external standards. However, she now looked beautiful and kind inside by the way she revealed herself. Elise gave Ryan a precious compliment by sharing a vulnerability of hers. Ryan wanted to protect her, rather than fight with her.

Elise Matthews continued, "Learning how to breathe is essential to living—living in peace, in joy, and having fun. Presence is about breathing and awareness. If you can learn to breathe—if you can learn how to exhale as well as inhale—you can experience life more fully. You can let go and let yourself be you."

"Miss Matthews, I know how to breathe," he replied sarcastically.

Elise saw many traits in Ryan she knew only too well in herself—arrogance, denial, judgment, anger, pride, and self-sufficiency. She took another path, "Mr. Edwards, I know you think this is a bit much. Think of it this way. There are eight emotional values, eight virtues, you can feel and use at any time. Try to access them whenever you find yourself off balance and circumstances are going against you. Run through these values in your mind. They are your guideposts. Practice as you would practice your passing drills. Let the values be present in your awareness—to help you, to calm you, to reassure you, and to strengthen you."

Ryan countered back, "It's awfully complicated."

"Not really, Mr. Edwards. It's simple to remember. It's a mnemonic. I designed it that way for you. Eight emotional values—one for each of the eight days of the week—Sunday through Sunday. Eight emotional values—one for each note of the key of C major—middle C through C again. Each day and each note represents a value—Humility, Discipline, Faith, Courage, Optimism, Kindness, Charity, and Presence. You can remember them either way—by the days of the week or the notes of the scale."

"Sunday, or middle C, is for Humility which is about perspective and acceptance—through recognizing that you are human, that you make mistakes all day, that others do too, and that you can't go it alone in life no matter how hard you try.

"Monday, or the note D, is for Discipline which is about visualization and practice—through creating picture destinations of your purpose and goals, getting on the right side of your brain, and developing daily practice routines to realize the visual movie you created for yourself in your mind.

"Tuesday, or the note E, is for Faith which is about belief and trust—through identifying what you believe and committing to those beliefs in the heat of the battle when tested, challenged, or tempted in situations. It's about trusting your beliefs under pressure.

"Wednesday, or the note F, is for Courage which is about choice and change—through choosing your thoughts, your feelings, your actions. Your thoughts influence your feelings. Your thoughts, with your feelings, influence your actions. Choose each thought, one positive thought over another negative thought, to feel better and act more positively.

"Thursday, or the note G, is for Optimism which is about attitude and hope—through finding a positive outlook and disposition. It's creating a positive attitude of action, of resilience and of renewal to start over again each day. Optimism generates hope—a hopeful view of the outcome and of the future.

"Friday, or the note A, is for Kindness which is about patience and gentleness—through showing empathy and compassion for yourself and for others. Be patient with yourself and with others in times of struggle. Be gentle with yourself and with others during times of challenge.

"Saturday, or the note B, is for Charity which is about sharing and forgiving—through giving attention, support, approval, encouragement, and reassurance. It means a willingness to share you and be vulnerable too. It means forgiving and being able to let go of the past—letting go of your mistakes and others' mistakes.

"Everyday, Sunday again, or the note C again, is for Presence which is about breathing and awareness—through being, surrendering, and letting go to what is. It means being right here, right now, non-judgmentally aware of the moment—living in, participating in, and observing in the moment."

Ryan Edwards felt puzzled. He wondered how he could remember and use these values? Maybe he would break them into pieces, eight pieces. Maybe he would just try. Maybe he would just practice. Ryan was still skeptical. This seemed stupid. Or was he overloaded with discomfort and resistance to change?

Elise picked it up now, "These eight emotional values can be your internal guideposts, your compass, to direct your thinking, your feeling, and your doing in any situation."

Elise Matthews stopped. You could hear the quiet. Ryan hung on every word she said. He took it in intuitively, intellectually, and emotionally. Ryan Edwards had just been tutored. In one sense, he was frustrated. In another, he didn't mind it at all. He was confused but energized.

Ryan commented, "Miss Matthews, I still don't know how I am going to use them."

Elise Matthews exhaled, fatigued herself. "Mr. Edwards, just try them out. Try pieces in different situations. Find one thing that works for you and build from there. Play with it. Syrus said, 'Practice is the best of all instructors.'

"Over time, you may come to value these eight emotional values, or other values you choose, and you may be able to use them to respond in any situation. Make these values part of your beliefs. Your beliefs influence your behaviors. Live these values as guideposts—thinking, feeling, doing in any situation."

Ryan again asked himself how he was going to remember the eight values. He was dejected with the thought. "Miss Matthews, thanks again, but I'm a little tired. The values are very nice, but I will not be able to remember any of this."

Elise Matthews sighed, taking a breath. "Mr. Edwards, let me put this in the context of a 'Playbook'—your personal Playbook."

Ryan chuckled. "My Playbook, Miss Matthews?" He stood up, about to leave.

"Yes, Mr. Edwards, your portable Playbook, for any condition or situation you encounter—on or off the field," Elise asserted without hesitation. "Think of it as your Playbook of life."

Elise Matthews gave a directive this time, "Now please, Mr. Edwards, sit down."

Ryan Edwards followed her command. "Yes, Miss Matthews."

CHAPTER 17

Playbook

"The longer I live, the more I realize the impact of attitude on my life. Attitude, to me, is more important than facts. It is more important than the past, the education, the money, than circumstances, than failure, than successes, than what other people think or say or do. It is more important than appearance, giftedness or skill. It will make or break a company…a church…a home. The remarkable thing is we have a choice every day regarding the attitude we will embrace for that day. We cannot change our past…we cannot change the fact that people will act in a certain way. We cannot change the inevitable. The only thing we can do is play on the one string we have, and that is our attitude. I am convinced that life is 10% what happens to me and 90% how I react to it. And so it is with you…we are in charge of our Attitudes."

Charles Swindoll

Elise Matthews went to the blackboard and thought for a moment. She turned around and looked at Ryan Edwards, then turned back to the blackboard. Then she began to write.

"Mr. Edwards, you can surely manage to remember a short Playbook?" Elise asked him. "You learn them all the time for football. The eight emotional values are core disciplines for each day of the eight-day week. They are the foundation of your Playbook. They set the context and are the rules of the game—a set of guidelines to help keep you on course—now and perhaps throughout your life."

Ryan shot back, "I always remember my playbooks, Miss Edwards."

"Good, now write this down," she countered. Slowly and methodically she wrote the following outline, on the blackboard. It looked like the work of a football coach at halftime of a very tight game.

Be The "Emotional Athlete" and "Think To Cope"

How you think affects the way you feel and what you do: it's the "think-feel-do" triangle

The Emotional Athlete's motto:

"ASPIRE NOW, VALUE SELF-ACCEPTANCE"

with "PACE"

PACE stands for 1) Path, 2) Aim, 3) Code, and 4) Energy

1) The Path is NOW

Be NOW in each moment—present and aware

Be NOW in each moment—follow the NOW path

2) The Aim is SELF-ACCEPTANCE

Develop an attitude of self-acceptance, an attitude of accepting others, and an attitude of accepting life as it comes your way

Accept yourself unconditionally in each moment so you can accept others as they are and can accept life as it is

Accept yourself through your own affirmations:

-I'm OK
-You're OK
-It's OK
-I'll be OK

-You'll be OK
-It'll be OK
-I'm OK with that
-I'm OK with what is right now

-What's there to worry about? Nothing right now
-What's the worst that can happen? Little right now
-What's the issue worth? Not much right now
-There's time
-It can wait
-I trust I'll get through this one too

-Yes I am, yes I can, and yes I will NOW
-I totally and completely accept myself as I am
-'Day by day in every way I'm getting better and better' Emile Coue
-'I feel healthy! I feel happy! I feel terrific!' W. Clement Stone
-I am confident and glad to be here
-I am grateful for three things today . . .

-You are not alone
-I am always with you
-Trust in God's will for you
-Trust in you as you are right now
-Be a river and flow with what is
-'Be the water and the wave' Thich Nhat Hahn

3) The Code is eight VALUES

Your values are your guideposts through life

The values you choose are the code by which you live

Your values are your compass in life

Know your values, feel your values, live your values:

>Sunday: Humility is about Perspective and Acceptance
>Monday: Discipline is about Visualization and Practice
>Tuesday: Faith is about Belief and Trust
>Wednesday: Courage is about Choice and Change
>Thursday: Optimism is about Attitude and Hope
>Friday: Kindness is about Patience and Gentleness
>Saturday: Charity is about Sharing and Forgiving
>Everyday: Presence is about Breathing and Awareness

4) The Energy is ASPIRE

ASPIRE to be an Emotional Athlete, present each moment

ASPIRE to Emotional Fitness as an Emotional Athlete

ASPIRE each moment. Win the next five minutes:

>Aware-fully breathe and perceive
>Spiritually believe and trust
>Physically choose and do
>Intellectually form and talk
>Relationally engage and connect
>Emotionally feel and identify

5) Summary

The Emotional Athlete develops Emotional Fitness through PACE

Become an Emotional Athlete for yourself and others in your life

Be an Emotional Athlete through daily ASPIRE practice routines

Be fit—aware-fully, spiritually, physically, intellectually, relationally, and emotionally

An Emotional Athlete resides in everyone who is willing and able to try

Think To Cope: think-feel-do helps unconditional self-acceptance

Find your PACE—develop your Playbook and emotional coping toolbox

You are responsible for your thinking—choose your attitude

Practice, practice, practice—choose the habit of practice

Determine what you believe and live according to those beliefs

Win the next five minutes with your attitude, outlook, and disposition

Elise Edwards returned the chalk to its tray attached to the board. She stood back looking at Ryan. He glanced at the board, then at Elise Matthews, then back at the board. He was amused, confused, scared, interested, and threatened—all in a collage of feelings.

Elise Matthews began, "Mr. Edwards, this is your Playbook. It's portable. It is easy to remember, using a few memory aides. Use pieces of the Playbook only as you need them in any given situation."

Ryan Edwards was awestruck. This was Elise Matthews the coach in action, the Emotional Athlete version, coaching the emotional game of life.

For a controlled, measured and intensely closed Elise Matthews, you could feel the emotion and passion in her voice for her deeply felt concept. Her conviction for the Emotional Athlete was contagious as a powerful flu. Ryan Edwards was beginning to catch her cold and didn't mind it. Maybe this was for real.

Elise Matthews made an impassioned plea to Ryan Edwards to let go, to surrender, to accept, to breathe, to exhale, to just be—to take the self-judging, self-criticizing, self-monitoring governor off his life engine.

Ryan's self-monitoring was tying him up. He was in a straitjacket of precision and perfection—using costumes and roles and masks to keep people at a distance.

Elise Matthews continued her case. "We like to be known as athletes in some way. Be an Emotional Athlete too. Every athlete has her PACE. The Playbook is the Emotional Athlete's life PACE and rhythm to life.

"The PACE of life—ASPIRE NOW, VALUE SELF-ACCEPTANCE.

"Try the PACE of life—try. Aspire to Emotional Fitness through unconditional self-acceptance now, mindfully aware moment by moment.

"The PACE of life is four components: Path, Aim, Code, Energy—reminders for NOW, SELF-ACCEPTANCE, VALUE, ASPIRE.

"The Path is your roadmap, NOW. Live in time zone now, not time zone before or time zone after, not time zone earlier or time zone later. Stay on the road NOW, each moment.

"The Aim is your destination, SELF-ACCEPTANCE. The goal is self-acceptance through positive affirmations. If you can accept yourself, you can more easily accept others and life as it is. Live in peace through acceptance—surrender, trust, and letting go.

"The Code is your foundation, eight emotional VALUES—one for each of eight days. They are your rules to rely on and your compass when you lose your way in adversity. They become your perspective for living life. Choose values that are right for you.

"The Energy, is your passion, ASPIRE to Emotional Fitness each moment. ASPIRE energy is your fuel and presence, moment by moment. Engage through six ASPIRE routines. Win the next five minutes:

> -aware-fully breathe and perceive: that is your armor and protection
> -spiritually believe and trust: focus on one belief, surrender, and let go to it
> -physically choose and do: be aware, make explicit choices, then act
> -intellectually form and talk: form your views, and opinions, affirm yourself
> -relationally engage and connect: listen, engage, and connect with others
> -emotionally feel and identify: identify, tolerate and accept your feelings

"ASPIRE to Emotional Fitness and become an Emotional Athlete—with aware-ful fitness, spiritual fitness, physical fitness, intellectual fitness, relationship fitness, emotional fitness. ASPIRE NOW, VALUE SELF-ACCEPTANCE.

"Learning any new skill feels mechanical at first. With practice, intuitive muscle memory will effortlessly take over. Emotional Fitness is a skill set too."

Elise Matthews paused. "Any questions, Mr. Edwards?"

Elise

Ryan absorbed her words. It was simple. It was portable. He could memorize it.

Ryan responded, "No, Miss Matthews."

Elise Matthews held Ryan's attention. "Then one last minute on affirmations and self-affirmations. It all starts with how you think. How you think determines the way you feel and what you do. Make positive affirmations and engage in positive self-talk.

"Positive affirmations of self-acceptance shape your self-beliefs. Positive affirmations of acceptance and self-acceptance fuel you— to think, to feel, and to do positively. Develop your own positive affirmations in your self-talk. Here are mine:

-I'm OK
-You're OK
-It's OK
-I'll be OK
-You'll be OK
-It'll be OK
-I'm OK with that
-I'm OK with what is right now

-What's there to worry about? Nothing right now
-What's the worst that can happen? Little right now
-What's the issue worth? Not much right now
-There's time
-It can wait
-I trust I'll get through this one too

-Yes I am, yes I can, and yes I will NOW
-I totally and completely accept myself as I am
-'Day by day in every way I'm getting better and better' Emile Coue
-'I feel healthy! I feel happy! I feel terrific!' W. Clement Stone

-I am confident and glad to be here
-I am grateful for three things today . . .

-You are not alone
-I am always with you
-Trust in God's will for you
-Trust in you as you are right now
-Be a river and flow with what is
-'Be the water and the wave' Thich Nhat Hahn"

Elise paused, "One affirmation is an emotional problem solving routine as well:

'Yes I am, yes I can, and yes I will NOW.'"

"It's a mnemonic and way to cope in difficult situations under emotional stress:

'Yes I am, yes I can, and yes I will NOW.'

>-embrace yourself ('YES' is the mnemonic for 'embrace yourself')
>-identify active moods ('I am' is for 'identify active moods')
>-encourage yourself ('YES' is for 'encourage yourself')
>-investigate causes and notions ('I can' is for 'investigate causes and notions')
>-analyze negate distortions ('and' is for 'analyze negate distortions')
>-esteem yourself ('YES' is for 'esteem yourself')
>-isolate worthy interpretations listen let go ('I will' is for 'isolate worthy interpretations listen let go')
>-negotiate an optimistic way ('NOW' is for 'negotiate an optimistic way')

"In a difficult situation— whether feeling overwhelmed by thoughts, moods and emotions, or feeling triggered by some thought, distress or disappointment—try this emotional problem solving routine and exercise. Figure out what is going on inside by listening to your self-talk, your feelings, your impulses, and your actions.

"What are you thinking that makes you feel the way you do?

"Mindfulness is pretty simple. It starts with awareness. You notice how you are feeling. Ask yourself how you feel—angry, fearful, calm, or sad—in the moment. Look back at your thoughts to understand why you feel as you do. Identify your feeling. Observe what you are thinking. Ask yourself what belief, assumption, perception, idea, notion, or thought is active in your mind, which is coloring your feelings. Adjust your thoughts with a more balanced perspective. Negotiate with your feelings: analyze, dispute, and reframe your thinking more realistically to feel better. Feel better to act better. Act positively.

"Your feelings follow your thoughts. Change your thoughts to change your feelings.

Elise summarized, pulling it all together, "'Think-feel-do.' It's the dance of life. Learn the dance. Dance the dance. Take charge of your life with a calm and confident knowing that you will be able to cope with whatever circumstances come your way."

CHAPTER 18

EMOTIONAL ARCHITECT

"The privilege of a lifetime is being who you are."
Joseph Campbell

Elise Matthews had just architected Ryan Edward's personal Playbook. The Emotional Athlete's PACE in life—ASPIRE NOW, VALUE SELF-ACCEPTANCE each moment.

Win the next five minutes with a positive attitude—ASPIRE to Emotional Fitness.

The Playbook would become Ryan's best weapon to cope with any situation.

To become an Emotional Athlete is to become the self-accepting athlete, the self-esteeming athlete. Self-esteem is a feeling, a feeling about oneself. It's a choice that you and you alone make about yourself—about your opinion of yourself.

The choices you make about what you think and believe determine how you feel, which determines what you do.

The Emotional Athlete develops a healthy self-accepting opinion of himself—endurance, strength and flexibility fit to cope under stress and adversity.

Elise was trying to help Ryan see that thinking determines feeling and doing. Thinking determines how well you cope with life's challenges.

Elise wanted Ryan to consider life as a trying game, not just a winning game—focusing more on the process in the moment and less on the outcome at the end.

Elise Matthews was Ryan's coach—his emotional coach. Elise Matthews was making a plea for Ryan Edwards to wake up. She urged him to observe his thoughts, assumptions, beliefs, and perceptions about himself and the world around him. She suggested he be aware of his feelings that resulted from the thoughts in his head.

She coached him to sit with and quietly embrace the discomfort of his unpleasant thoughts and feelings—suggesting that he consciously accept his painful thoughts and feelings as they are—letting them flow right through him—like a thunder storm passing through a town, followed by the sun again. She urged him to begin again.

The Emotional Athlete is the coping athlete who is able to embrace the pain of distressing thoughts and feelings, without being knocked off balance and acting out destructively through drugs, alcohol, sex, gambling, eating or any other addiction, to escape pain and medicate difficult feelings.

The Emotional Athlete is the one who can cut himself slack in life, instead of performing emotional self-crucifixions for not measuring up to unrealistic, self-imposed standards.

Ryan replayed her words and knew she was telling her own story. She was getting very personal in revealing herself. "'Never good enough' is a rough way to live—one that can lead to all sorts of addictions, escapes and refuge places to free oneself of the emotional pain of never measuring up to oneself. The escape behaviors to medicate pain and manage feelings of self-loathing don't work. Trust me. I know. I tried them. That was my life.

"Nothing can fill the void inside yourself without self-acceptance that comes with surrender and letting go to something bigger than you. The 'never enough' or 'not good enough' syndrome is a distortion in one's mind and internal reality. A person's reality is created by his core beliefs about himself, his beliefs about others and his beliefs about the world.

"The Emotional Athlete, however, becomes aware of his self-imposed madness and changes the game by changing his beliefs. It isn't easy. It takes disciplined, repetitive, daily practice to acquire and maintain acceptance skills and to change beliefs.

"Self-acceptance is a counterintuitive path leading to acceptance of life and others as they are. Maybe you can arrive at acceptance without a self-acceptance stop first. But I had to take the self-acceptance path. It's what worked for me. I learned to like myself."

Ryan looked at Elise Matthews. She glowed with a brilliant poise. Her presence filled the room. Ryan stared in reverence. She was inside Ryan's emotional life by exposing her own at great risk. It was an act of courage sharing her emotions.

Ryan tried to stop her. "Miss Matthews, why are you sharing this with me?"

Elise ducked his penetrating question. "Maybe, Mr. Edwards, there's another way to look at it. Try to think about it this way. When you throw a pass, are you worried about the mechanics of your pass from windup to release? Hardly, you cock your arm and let it rip with

Elise

confidence, with a trusting eye toward the finish. You merely focus on the follow-through. You know that if your follow-through is OK, the rest of your throw is OK. You see a successful pass in advance. You are not self-monitoring your throwing motion.

The same principle applies in other sports. In basketball, you focus on the finish of your shot. In tennis, you focus on the follow-through of your stroke. In golf, you focus on the finish in your swing. Get the follow-through right, and the shot generally turns out OK."

Ryan was confident. "I'm with you, Miss Matthews. Why are you sharing this with me?"

Elise Matthews ducked Ryan's question again, "The same principle applies to the Emotional Athlete. The Emotional Athlete's follow-through is unconditional self-acceptance. Get the self-acceptance follow-through right. The rest will be OK too.

"The Emotional Athlete's follow-through is unconditional self-acceptance right now.

"He knows he is OK. He knows it is OK. He knows others are OK—right now."

Ryan Edwards interrupted with some force, "Miss Matthews, how do you know this to be true with such confidence? And why are you sharing this with me?" His question was ironic coming from one who lived and bluffed his way through life.

Elise smiled. She was strong, solid, and firmly grounded. Yet she was anything but a tree. She was a goddess. "Mr. Edwards, I am trying to protect you from living your life as I have lived mine."

Ryan swallowed hard, losing his breath. Elise Matthews cared for him. He tried to maintain his composure and hold back a tear. Ryan

Edwards never cried. Crying was illegal in his family—a fifteen-yard penalty at a minimum.

"So, Miss Matthews, why are you telling me this?"

Elise took a breath. "Mr. Edwards, because I want to help you and protect you from yourself. I wish I had someone who could have done that for me."

There was a deadening silence. Ryan Edwards was utterly moved.

Elise continued, "This Playbook—it's my approach. It works for me. You and I are similar. I took a chance. I took a risk. Perhaps I am wrong to interfere. I couldn't help myself. I see me in you, and I don't want you to go through my pain and my suffering. I am once again trying to control what I shouldn't—this time it's you.

"I guess I could have left you alone and let you figure it out on your own. You would have, eventually through your own experiences. But I had to try. And now that I have tried, I will try to let it go and surrender."

Elise Matthews's confession continued. Ryan wondered if she had ever been this open with anyone in her life, even her ex-boyfriend. Ex-boyfriend. What happened there? Everyone knew she had a serious boyfriend. But nobody knew what happened.

"I try to control everything in my life. I think that I can guarantee outcomes. Whatever I do, whatever the outcome, no matter how well I perform, it's not good enough. When I look in the mirror, I'm not good enough for me, in my own view. I look outside to others for their approval, affirmation, and assurance to prove to myself that I am good enough in my own eyes. I need to and try to be perfect and try to play the perfect game with unrealistic precision. It's perfection—always and everywhere. That's my Achilles heel.

Elise

"I go to Mass each week to remind myself to let go, to surrender, to believe, to trust, and to accept. Sometimes, I am able to surrender and let go—surrender to God, in my case. Sometimes I am not.

"When I am in church, I try to be more human and cut myself some slack for making mistakes. When I can do this, I can exhale, not just inhale.

"One reason I go to church—it's one of the few places I can really exhale and let go. It's always been a place I have felt safe enough to do so. It reminds me of home base when I was a kid playing the game 'capture the flag.' You feel safe when you touch home base. Church is my home base—where I can go when I'm scared and alone.

"Mr. Edwards, I am not trying to teach, lecture, or reproach you, though I'm sure it comes off that way. I am only trying to help you, because I am a little scared for you. I don't want you to take my path. I don't want you to end up as I have."

"The truth is, Mr. Edwards, that I blew it. I really blew it. I tried to go it alone. I never asked for help. I never let anyone in my world. I don't want the same for you. I have tried to protect you from yourself, as I wish someone had tried to protect me. I had to try with you, Mr. Edwards. Don't ask me why? Because I don't know the answer to that one."

Elise Matthews stopped speaking. Ryan looked at her in silence and gratitude. He too was in constant emotional pain and agitation—believing that he was never good enough.

Things weren't working for him as smoothly as he portrayed externally. His internal emotional house was in chaos and disarray. His self-focus and absorption were self-preservation for his Achilles heel—his low self-esteem based on his core belief that he wasn't good enough.

"You seem to have the all answers Miss Matthews," Ryan was scared. Out of self-defense and nervousness of being found out, he challenged her.

"I have the answers for myself. I know what works for me. Find what work for you. If my experience is helpful, then I am happy for you." She stopped with a long pause. In a soft and gentle tone she continued, "Focus on the follow-through of life—be an Emotional Athlete, ASPIRE NOW, VALUE SELF-ACCEPTANCE—toward Emotional Fitness to be your trusting, self-respecting, self-esteeming, self-accepting you—anywhere, anytime. It's simply 'being free to be OK being just me.'"

Elise Matthews was on a role—a heatedly passionate and cathartic role. She looked cool, strong, hot, and in command, in her sexy tan cotton dress. She was elegantly simple, elegantly pure. Ryan Edwards was getting schooled in character development. Elise Matthews was sexy and tough—character tough, humility tough, values tough, self-acceptance tough. Elise Matthews was living proof that integrity is sexy.

"Mr. Edwards, no matter the level or degree of external performance-based success or fame or fortune a person may experience, the essential follow-through in life is the same for everyone—simply be OK as you are right now.

"Focus on your own follow-through, Mr. Edwards. Focus on your self-acceptance when you look in the mirror. Shape, paint and repaint your identity throughout life. It's your Playbook for life, Mr. Edwards—the Emotional Athlete's 'PACE' is 'ASPIRE NOW, VALUE SELF-ACCEPTANCE.'

"ASPIRE to Emotional Fitness being just you.

"Trust the ASPIRE process in each moment, and control the process in the moment. Surrender and let go of the outcome—which is out of your control. Let go of yesterday. Surrender tomorrow. Have faith in today NOW. Trust the process of living in the moment by being present. Believe in your picture destinations with hope.

"Control your thoughts, stop fighting what is and just accept life as it comes. Control the process, but surrender the outcome. If you want to control something, then control the process in the moment. Control your thoughts, control your assumptions, control your beliefs, control your notions, control your perceptions, control your disposition, control your view, control your awareness, control your decisions, control your reactions, control your responses, control your self-acceptance, control your acceptance of what is NOW, control your gratitude, control your faith. Control your attitudes.

"It's counterintuitive Mr. Edwards. Self-acceptance will get you out of yourself. It will get you unstuck from isolation and get you re-engaged in the world with others.

Self-acceptance takes you out of the picture and puts others more in the picture.

"Self-acceptance is a way out of yourself, Mr. Edwards."

CHAPTER 19

ELISE MATTHEWS

"There is nothing either good or bad, but thinking makes it so."

Shakespeare

Elise pressed on as Ryan took it in, "Win the next five minutes—ASPIRE to Emotional Fitness each moment. Mr. Edwards, decide what works for you."

Ryan looked back on his life. He put enormous pressure on himself no matter what the situation or what he achieved. There was always something else and always something more. Who he was and what he had done was never quite good enough. He felt relieved in a way just thinking about Elise's Playbook. A little more self-acceptance was a freeing notion. He soaked in Elise Matthews's words with a respect that he never afforded any other teacher or coach. And Elise Matthews was just the stupid music teacher!

Elise came to a close. "Mr. Edwards, Think To Cope. The PACE of life is a Playbook for the Emotional Athlete toward Emotional Fitness—to think, to feel, and to do better."

Ryan was reflecting in Room 101 as he replayed the words she spoke. Elise Edwards created this Playbook just for him—to become an Emotional Athlete. Ryan thought that Elise Matthews might just be the best offensive line protecting him that he would ever have. She was a gift. Elise Matthews was Ryan Edwards. She was a female version.

Elise had similar experiences and seemed to know where Ryan was headed. She was caught cheating in high school on a test because "she had to get an A." Elise put so much pressure on herself, she lost all perspective, winning at all costs and following the lead of her ultra-competitive peers. Elise lost her way and her compass.

Her coaches rescued her, bailing her out to avoid expulsion. The high school principal wanted her gone. He had it in for her, because Elise Matthews thought she was special. Beautiful, smart, outgoing, athletic—she had it all, except humility. Her arrogance was a cover for her slight semblance of self-respect. She afforded herself little self-appreciation.

Elise Matthews was anything but OK on the inside with Elise Matthews. Yet outwardly, everyone thought she had it all going her way. No one would have imagined Elise had any struggles inside herself. To others, it seemed she glided through life effortlessly with the wind always at her back—until it all changed.

Elise Matthews became a pothead her sophomore year in high school and drank to cope with her problems. She smoked and drank to relieve her pain, to manage her unwanted feelings, and to relieve her emotional pain. She hid her abuse and her addiction from most everyone, except from herself.

The more she acted out, the worse she felt about herself. No one would have ever imagined her severe and deep self-loathing. She'd drink and drive, getting picked up by the police on several occasions. But that was the 1960s, and she could charm her way out of trouble, getting the police to lead her home as she followed driving her own car.

Her coaches caught wind of this. They saved her again. They finally gave her an ultimatum. Unless she would start to help herself, they would no longer help her. So Elise Matthews quietly went to rehab for a month and then another month. She joined AA; she was seventeen years old. Her coaches sponsored her for several years during her early recovery.

Her parents were essentially absent. Her mother drank too much, an alcoholic herself, so there was no interest in addressing alcohol abuse and addiction. That would make it a family problem, and her mother had no interest in changing her behavior. The story was similar in Ryan's family as well. His parents were absent, alcohol addiction was all over his family, and problems were always swept under the rug as if they didn't exist.

Who would have guessed that Elise Matthews had any problems? How did she keep such a secret? What pain she must have had in hiding it. She was so accomplished, attractive, athletic, popular, seductive, and talented in every way. Elise Matthews was always on camera, always hiding her self-doubts and self-deprecation. Yet she had no one to turn to. It was forbidden to reveal that she was vulnerable or in pain or that she needed help.

Elise Matthews was alone inside herself, often isolating herself in ways she didn't realize. She did everything on her own, self-sufficiently, to prove to herself that she measured up in her own eyes and in the judgmental eyes of others to whom she gave the power to approve or disapprove of her performance. This was a trap of her own making based on her wrongly calibrated self-beliefs. She let others decide if she was worthy, adequate, lovable, or OK. She never asked herself if she was OK enough, she never valued her own opinion of herself. She decided to let other people decide for her if she was OK enough.

And she would never ask for help. How embarrassing, only losers ask for help, only the weak ask for help. Only the pathetic need others. Self-sufficiency is the gold standard. Until you crash and you are all alone.

Ryan now realized that Elise, too, was alone inside herself. It hadn't occurred to him until now. Ryan was surprised with himself for making this observation. It required that he look outside himself and step into another person's shoes with empathy. Ryan was off balance, and a rush of emotions overcame him.

This was a new Ryan Edwards—to feel anything at all—having never felt much of anything in his life. He always avoided and ran away from his emotions. Ryan's emotions absolutely frightened him. He distrusted them. And his parents taught him to stuff and repress all emotions, that everything was OK without emotions. That was a delusional belief. He lived a completely stoic existence through a simple and stoic routine—set a goal, practice, prepare, perform, achieve. Think it, do it, but *never* feel it. Ryan Edwards never allowed himself to feel anything. In thinking and doing he always was safe.

If the waltz of living life was "think-feel-do," then Ryan Edwards rewrote the dance of life into a two-step "think-do" "think-do," "think-do"—like clockwork in execution. Ryan Edwards, the quintessential "think-do" guy, did not realize that when he met true adversity in his "think-do" world, he would get stuck in an emotionally paralytic ditch. He tried to deny his feelings, but they finally caught up with him. The pain and injuries were becoming too much to ignore. His acting out through drinking, temporarily soothing his painful feelings, had lost its power. Acting out was destructive now, making things worse each time.

His feelings of pain, rejection, and isolation—which he would never share—paralyzed him in emotional quicksand. He sometimes found himself for no apparent reason obsessively stuck up inside his head—paralyzed in procrastination and fear of action.

According to Elise Matthews, the Emotional Athlete was at her best in the heat of the athletic contest of life's challenges—taking her emotional temperature and embracing it. Aware of the situation, thinking affirmatively, she would act positively and keep moving.

The triangle offense—think-feel-do—helped her get unstuck. Elise Matthews encouraged him again. "Mr. Edwards, 'win the next five minutes.' Forget the last five minutes. Think-feel-do, acknowledge, embrace, and accept your feelings and get moving again. Embrace painful feelings and emotional injuries—feel it to heal it; share it to repair it."

Elise Matthews wasn't done. "It's the difference, Mr. Edwards, between knowing and wondering in an emotionally athletic sort of way, knowing that 'I'm OK as I am.'"

Elise Matthews paused to see if Ryan was following. "Mr. Edwards, one test is to ask yourself some questions. For instance, if you feel rejected, was it because of someone else or did you reject yourself in the situation? And for respect, if you don't think you receive the respect you deserve, ask yourself if you are giving yourself enough self-respect? And for esteem and worth, if you believe you are not being valued the way you should by others, ask yourself are you truly being supportive of your own self-worth?"

Ryan interrupted, "That's not true." He was full of resistance and denial. She hit a nerve. He constantly rejected, judged, and criticized himself. Ryan was sensitive to feedback—emotionally raw and vulnerable because he wasn't good enough for himself.

"It all starts inside ourselves. We are the problem and the solution," Elise maintained, "Sheldon Kopp said, 'All of the significant battles are waged within the self.' We send out what we believe about ourselves and how we self-identify.

"Acceptance begins with self-acceptance. Respect begins with self-respect. Trust begins with self-trust. Hope begins with self-hope. Esteem begins with self-esteem. Forgiveness of others begins with self-forgiveness. Life is an inside-out game, Mr. Edwards.

"Set the tone, and others will mirror your tone back to you—others will follow your lead."

Elise was again finding her stride. "People mirror back to us only what we already believe and say about ourselves. Acceptance starts inside; acceptance starts with self-acceptance.

"The responses you receive from others follow your internal perceptions of yourself. Rather than yield control to others, trying to manage their opinions of you, take control with your self-acceptance lever. Control in life lies in one's attitude of self-acceptance.

"It's a little ironic that we all try to control the external events, ignoring the internal events. The only control panel and dashboard one can affect is that of one's internal self-beliefs and one's attitudes. Depend on the approval and affirmation of others for your self-worth, and you are a human Ping-Pong ball, having no control—trying to please others and guarantee outcomes, performances, impressions and relationships.

"Mr. Edwards, focus on the follow-through—your own unconditional, non-contingent self-acceptance now, moment by moment. It will become a habit. Other challenges in your world—obsessive thinking, compulsive doing, anxiety, depression, addiction, low self-esteem, social anxiety, poor concentration, and procrastination—may become less debilitating, less threatening and less oppressive.

"Good is good enough. ASPIRE NOW, VALUE SELF-ACCEPTANCE. Feel better about yourself and your circumstances in life.

"Come to self-acceptance as a way of life, and your voices up inside your head may just quiet. Your anxieties, your fears, your worries, and your doubts may lessen. Your addictive thinking, feeling and behaving may diminish. Your depressive moods may lift.

One move toward unconditional self-acceptance—'I'm OK as I am'—this one thought, this one picture, may help you change your life forever.

"And, Mr. Edwards, now we are done."

Ryan felt robbed. He oddly wanted more. He felt a soothing, calming, safe sensation while listening to Elise Matthews describing how he could become his own best friend.

She let it sink in. "At the end of the day, Mr. Edwards, you are either on your own side—in any situation—or you are not. ASPIRE NOW, VALUE SELF-ACCEPTANCE—it may help. Try it. You have nothing to lose.

"Focus on the follow-through, 'I am on my own side right now, I accept myself as I am, I am OK being me as I am right now.' It's simple, Mr. Edwards, simple positive self-talk.

"Good athletes do it in their sports all the time. The degree you can do this under pressure, stress, or setbacks is the difference between the 25-handicap Emotional Athlete and the 5-handicap Emotional Athlete. Daily practice, daily routines, daily preparation."

"Miss Matthews, you seem have it all figured out," Ryan said with a sigh. He was defenseless. He felt vulnerable—about becoming an Emotional Athlete. She hit emotional nerves through Ryan's seemingly fearless exterior.

She addressed his crack, "No, Mr. Edwards, 'I don't have it figured out.' Like you, I thought I did, but I don't. The only thing I figured out is that without my own self-acceptance, life is a miserable game to play.

"When I abdicate my self-worth, my self-esteem, my self-concept to the opinions and judgments of others for approval and validation, I am painfully lost and rudderless."

Ryan felt threatened with her view of life. He was scared. "And how, Miss Matthews, did you 'do it,' suddenly finding this self-acceptance?"

She swallowed, reminding herself that she would have done the same thing in his shoes at his age. She gathered all the patience and tolerance she could muster. "Mr. Edwards, I didn't just 'do it,' as you suggest. But I did find it. I tried every way I could to 'do it'—all on my own. But it didn't work. I was alone. I gave up. I surrendered. And that's when I 'found it'—when I finally let go and accepted myself as I am right now.

"Ryan regretted his insulting questions. He was anxious and scared. He caught himself and apologized. "I'm sorry, Miss Matthews."

Elise caught his apology, "But of course, Mr. Edwards, this approach isn't for everyone. It works for me. It may not be for you. Ask yourself, is it all working for you? If it is, then forget everything I said. That's your choice.

"You are your own architect for becoming your own Emotional Athlete."

What Elise Matthews knew for herself was that changing her thinking and changing her doing in positive ways was also changing her brain paths.

Changes in her thinking and doing were cognitively restructuring her brain responses and defaults. Her new thinking habits positively changed her feelings and doings—without medication.

But Emotional Fitness also comes at a price—hard work and daily practice of the Playbook. There are no shortcuts; there is daily maintenance, training and practice.

With that, Elise Matthews walked out of Room 101 for the final time. There would be no more sessions like those of the preceding days. Ryan was debating with himself whether it was Elise Matthews or Vince Lombardi who left the room. She was passionate about her belief in the Emotional Athlete and Emotional Fitness, delivering a heartfelt message to him. Ryan Edwards now realized how much he was like Elise Matthews. Awake in a new way, Ryan was aware, alert, and absorbed in the present for the first time.

It was game time now. Ryan was challenged to step it up emotionally by his unsuspecting music teacher. Who would have guessed? Would he accept her challenge?

Touched, Ryan Edwards was holding back tears. He had never cried before. No one had ever done anything this nice or thoughtful for him before. He too, like Elise Matthews, was living all alone inside himself—he was a lone wolf who thought he could essentially go it alone, self-sufficiently and without the need or aid of others.

Elise Edwards was warning him not to make the same mistakes she had made—that it is impossible to go it alone. Everyone needs other people in their lives. Elise Matthews wanted to save Ryan Edwards from his arrogant, cocky, solo self. Elise Matthews knew what it was like to be alone. She was all alone and hated being there.

Ryan Edwards broke down in tears.

CHAPTER 20

Ryan Edwards

"Do what you can, with what you have, where you are."
Theodore Roosevelt

Ryan Edwards was the last of four children. For all outward appearances, he was from a very successful family. But Ryan Edwards was alone. He grew up abandoned. He performed his way through childhood striving for any attention he could get. Ryan Edwards was the living definition of "the invisible man." He went unnoticed at home, so he gravitated to his friends, playing sports constantly, doing well in school, courting the girls, performing his way through life in order to prove himself to himself in order to like himself from moment to moment.

Still sitting in his seat, alone now in Room 101, Ryan Edwards wiped the tears from his cheek. He reflected more on Elise Matthews's words.

Ryan Edwards often found himself stuck up inside his head, obsessing, replaying and ruminating, again and again. Ryan suffered from OCD. He couldn't stop thinking unless he made himself aware of it or he changed activities.

"Mr. Edwards, your beliefs drive who you are—you are your self-beliefs, consciously and unconsciously. Your beliefs are your lens, your perspective, and your filter for how you react and for what you think, feel, do, perceive, remember, imagine, and experience."

Ryan repeated Elise Matthews's mantra again and again. "Accept that you are good enough right now. When you are OK enough for yourself, you can accept others and accept things as they are. Be you—be OK enough as you are right now.

"Self-acceptance now is 'I'm OK enough as I am right now.' It fuels and renews you with affirmation, assurance, appreciation, and acknowledgment.

"How you think is everything, Think To Cope, Mr. Edwards. Your thinking ignites your feeling and doing. Think To Cope, Mr. Edwards. Get your self-beliefs right for you. Reform your self-beliefs—re-view them, restructure them, repair them, renew them.

"Stop fighting yourself and give in to you as you are. Be OK with you as you are—be enough as you are. Wake up. You are there already."

Her voice was clear and strong in his mind. He obsessively replayed her words in his mind again and again. "Free yourself from your self-imposed prison of self-judgment— shackled to masks, mirrors, costumes, and walls of your carefully self-constructed prison—with the purpose of proving to yourself that you are perfect.

"Faith is knowing now—knowing you're OK now as you are through self-acceptance.

"Faith now is acceptance now—non-judgment, non-opinion, non-interpretation, non-competition, non-criticism, non-comparison, non-conclusion, non-evaluation of oneself.

Elise

"Self-acceptance is the engine and the destination. It's your follow-through."

Ryan paused a moment in a black, empty awareness. He picked it up at a different point in the film. Elise continued talking in his mind, "Mr. Edwards, I am amused. You smirk, but in the absence of positive self-beliefs and affirmations, you may have a different set of beliefs and self-talk thoughts—perhaps negative ones—going on inside your head. You just may not realize it.

"Negative unconscious beliefs and negative automatic thoughts go like this, 'I am a failure, I'm a loser, I'm not attractive, I'm not good enough, I'm not perfect, or I am worthless.'

"Positive conscious beliefs and positive automatic thoughts go like this, 'I'm OK as I am.' 'Whatever mistakes I make, I totally and completely accept myself.'

"The choice of self-beliefs is your choice of attitude toward yourself."

Ryan's smirk shifted to a look of terror. He felt like a fraud. The horror was that Elise Matthews was right. In spite of all of Ryan Edwards's outward successes again and again on and off the field, he still continued to struggle, having strong self-downing thoughts.

When he threw an interception—even though he was a candidate to be all-state quarterback—he often downed himself saying, "I am a loser, I hate myself." When he couldn't seem to grasp a calculus concept that was easy for everyone else, he would say, "I am so stupid." When he got a rejection letter from a school, even though he was a top quarterback in the nation, he would tell himself, "I'm worthless."

When Ryan failed to meet his mark in any specific situation, he downed himself as his first reaction, beating himself up as his default response.

His self-reflective nightmare was interrupted with another scene replaying in his mind. "Mr. Edwards, snap out of it. It's OK. You're OK. You are not perfect. You are flawed—like everyone else—because you're human. Relax. You'll never be perfect.

"Quit trying to be perfect. Try for perfect acceptance—of yourself, of others, of life itself.

"You are not the only one performing this madness." What madness? His OCD created mental pain that caused him to act out and escape his anguish through addictive coping behaviors. Alcohol was a growing pain relief and mental coping crutch. He was managing his feelings and medicating his pain through more and more alcohol and binge drinking. Elise Matthews stepped in at a fortunate time for Ryan.

Did Elise Matthews know that alcohol was his next stop? "I tried alcohol as a solution to manage anxiety and painful feelings. It didn't work.

"After the game yesterday, you probably had some injuries, like a strained hamstring. What did you do? You rested it. You went through physical therapy to heal and recover your muscles. But did you really tell yourself you are a loser because you pulled a hamstring as a result of leading six scoring drives to win a big game? Hardly.

"Whether you know it or not, you may have pulled several 'emotional hamstrings' over the years, if not broken several 'emotional bones,' one of which someday may feel like your heart. You acquired these emotional injuries as a result of the 'emotional hits' you have sustained during your life—those hits from growing up in your family, those hits as a cost of your efforts, achievements, and setbacks, and those hits you have experienced because you had the courage to try and fail.

"Why, Mr. Edwards, would you ever go back on the 'emotional football field' injured, when you have the opportunity to repair your emotional injuries through The Playbook or some other coping routines that work for you?

"Why wouldn't you go through an 'emotional rehab routine' by developing a positive set of emotional beliefs, like the eight emotional values? Why wouldn't you replace the emotional, self-downing injuries that you have left unaddressed for years? Why not replace the negative self-talk—'I am such a loser because I failed to meet my expectation,' with a positive affirmation—'I am OK right now as I am?'

"You wouldn't avoid rehab in football. So why would you avoid emotional rehab in your everyday life, throughout your daily fifty thousand breaths and thoughts where you are playing the game of life each moment?"

Elise Matthews paused, compassionately responding to her own question, "You wouldn't, Mr. Edwards, would you?" Ever strong, ever powerful, Ryan Edwards sheepishly shook his head "no" like a little boy of five years might shake his head to his mother.

"So, Mr. Edwards," Elise Matthews concluded, "Here's a choice to consider. If you choose to embrace these eight emotional beliefs as values, if you translate these beliefs into affirmations, if you mentally rewrite over old emotional injuries and negative beliefs with new, positive beliefs each day—then maybe you will consider saying these affirmations or a set of affirmations that work for you.

"If you are going to live so much up inside your head with your OCD, can you at least be positive about it? You might find through practice of The Playbook routines that your mind quiets over time—that peace, joy, happiness, accomplishment, and service come a little bit easier. You may find your relationships improve."

Ryan again cut to another portion of this mental game tape, replaying another scene, "And for the semester, what can I expect for my grade, Miss Matthews?"

Elise Matthews was exhausted with Ryan's self-centered question. She had revealed much of her inner life and struggles. She wasn't sure how much of it, if any, would stick with him. She took a new approach, letting go and surrendering herself. "As of today, Mr. Edwards, you will receive an A for the semester, no strings attached."

Ryan Edwards was stunned with disbelief. "Miss Matthews, I don't have to do anything for the rest of the semester? But why?"

Elise Matthews confirmed back, "Yes, you have nothing more to do this semester."

Ryan Edwards pressed for more details, "What about my piano recital in December?"

Elise sighed. "I'm sure someone as talented as you can pull off 'Mary had a Little Lamb.'"

Elise saw the adolescence still in him. "This class, Mr. Edwards, is not about a grade from a meaningless music teacher, who you will never see again.

"These eight extra sessions are about grading yourself, each day, using the VALUES code, the SELF-ACCEPTANCE aim, the ASPIRE energy, the NOW path.

"Life is a 'HARD' choice—humility and acceptance or resistance and denial.

Choose humility and acceptance over resistance and denial. Make the HARD choice.

"One of the difficult parts of life, Mr. Edwards, is self-grading. No one else can grade you but you. This can feel cruel and unsettling or invigorating and freeing. We each grade ourselves, whether we are eighteen or eighty years old. No one can grade you but you. The sooner you learn this, the more peaceful and fulfilling your life will be."

Ryan later learned that Elise Matthews made the HARD choice during rehab for alcohol abuse. Elise drank to cope with her anxiety and inability to be nice to herself—pursuing perfection to prove her worth to herself—achievement by achievement.

But how could that be? Rehab was for losers—not for a high-performing, hot, rock-star student athlete who seemingly had it all going for her. You had to be pathetic to go to rehab, yet Elise Matthews was anything but pathetic. How could that be? She had an alcohol addiction and went to AA. But Elise Matthews was anything but a loser.

Ryan Edwards also learned that Elise Matthews trained herself to substitute her addictive thinking, feeling, and doing for healthy ASPIRE cognitive habits and self-acceptance affirmations from The Playbook. Elise created 'emotional rehab' routines for her low self-esteem, her perfectionism, her 'never good enough' beliefs, and her OCD.

She had developed into an Emotional Athlete through hard work and persistence. She pursued Emotional Fitness in her life. Over time she experienced more peace, mental quiet, self-confidence, self-worth, and happiness in her life—unattached to outcomes.

The "think-feel-do drugs" she used were the "cognitive drugs" of—self-acceptance, acceptance of others, acceptance of life as it is, surrender, letting go, non-resistance, non-attachment, non-judgment, faith, belief, trust, hope, positive attitude, optimism, humility, compassion, empathy, patience, tolerance, action, motion, kindness, breathing, slowing down, awareness, doing one thing at a time, presence each moment, humor, and gratitude.

Somewhere she received the grace to see and embrace in a 'judo move' her personality and chemistry—turning the addictive and OCD forces working against her to her advantage—through acceptance, surrender, and letting go. She substituted her destructive and abusive mental addictions for a set of positive thinking, feeling, and doing addictions—starting with unconditional self-acceptance.

Ryan recalled more, "Mr. Edwards, cheating is really self-cheating. There's a lot of temptation out there because others you know cheat and seem to get away with it.

"But here is the deal with cheating. When you cheat, there is no one you cheat more than you. The person you hurt the most, maybe not today, but tomorrow, is you. The scars and the wounds of cheating don't just dissolve on their own. They simply look back at you in the mirror, as Dorian Gray discovered. You alone are the one you wound when you cheat.

"Cheating or not cheating tells you everything about yourself—how you think about yourself—how you respect or disrespect yourself, whether you have confidence in yourself or not, how you esteem yourself or devalue yourself. Cheating tells you how kind, patient, and gentle you are towards yourself.

"Cheating is a choice. Your decision when challenged with the temptation, large or small, first makes a statement about you to yourself. When you cheat, you feel 'I'm NOT OK with me as I am.' The residual pain of 'successful cheating' lingers and deepens like a cancer over time. There is no perfect crime of dishonesty. Trust me on this one. I know.

"Recognize and be aware that you are always painting your own canvas with the decisions you make day in and day out—adding to your story—simplifying it or complicating it, building it or destroying it, using bright colors of the rainbow or dark shades of black and gray."

Elise Matthews came in again for another passionate close to try to persuade Ryan Edwards to make some changes in his life. "You are the artist, the painter, the architect, the author of your own life. Don't take that responsibility lightly. Edit your story, healing yourself each day with each new choice you make. It depends on how you think about it. Think To Cope. It's your choice how you choose to think.

"Mr. Edwards, try to build a bridge, a relationship, a connection to yourself—construct it with the steel material of character and integrity filled with of humility, discipline, faith, courage, optimism, kindness, charity, and presence.

"Build bridges to others as well. Take yourself out of the picture and look outside. You'll begin to forget yourself when you can accept yourself."

Elise Matthews ended skeptically. She doubted that Ryan Edwards would embrace any of the Playbook, "Mr. Edwards, we are now finished. I know that you think classical music is for the not-so-athletic person. But you can manage the recital playing 'Mary had a Little Lamb' with your social following and presence. Everyone will cut the football star some slack."

Ryan Edwards was stung. "Miss Matthews, that was a cheap shot."

Elise Matthews held her ground. "Mr. Edwards, it is you who makes fun of yourself. If you still feel hurt, I have a music suggestion—listen to Vivaldi. Vivaldi will always be there when you are struggling and hurting. Music, classical music, can heal you. Vivaldi can always pick you up. When you need more, try Corelli, Telemann, Bach, or Mozart. They are your friends too.

"Remember, Mr. Edwards, Vivaldi is always there for you."

Ryan Edwards had one more question, "Miss Matthews, why, why me?"

Elise Matthews answered in surprise, "Mr. Edwards, that's a most provocative question."

Ryan Edwards was impatiently waiting now. "Yes?"

Elise Matthews then asked, "Mr. Edwards, do you know anything about starfish?"

Ryan replied sarcastically, "I don't go to the beach much. It would wreck my shoes."

Elise was hurt. She sighed and concluded, "Mr. Edwards, what if I told you I just might be your starfish thrower." Elise Matthews left Room 101 one final time.

Ryan was laughing at this image. "What the hel…what is a starfish thrower?"

Elise Matthews stopped in her heels, late for Mass. "Mr. Edwards. It's up to you now. Good luck." Elise Matthews walked out of Room 101 for the last time. Ryan Edwards was scared—he never felt so alone, insecure, unsure, inadequate, and lost inside.

CHAPTER 21

REVIEW

> "The greatest way to live with honor in this world is to be what we pretend to be."
>
> — **Socrates**

Ryan Edwards was obsessed. He wanted to know more. He wanted to change. Ryan drifted back to the Playbook and the Emotional Athlete's PACE of life—PATH, AIM, CODE, and ENERGY. ASPIRE NOW, VALUE SELF-ACCEPTANCE.

The PATH is NOW. The only moment is NOW. Living in the past with regret, guilt, shame, and anger causes despair. Living in the future with doubt, anxiety, fear, and worry causes distress. The only place to be is in time zone NOW—in contrast to time zone EARLIER or time zone LATER. There is no fear NOW.

The AIM is SELF-ACCEPTANCE—it's a destination to heal and to grow, to share and to contribute, to develop relationships, to look outside you and engage in the world.

The CODE is eight VALUES—the values inside each of us to live by each day—to keep on course. They are the rules of the road—your guide and your compass in life:

-Humility Sunday, or middle C, is the ability to see with perspective one's limitations. Humility reminds us that we aren't perfect, we are human, we make mistakes daily, and there is someone greater than us. We can't go it alone. We need other people in our lives.

-Discipline Monday, or the note D, is the ability to visualize a destination. Discipline is a compass through picture destinations. Discipline is practice to focus and grow toward visual movies. The mental movies are emotional passion to motivate you.

-Faith Tuesday, or the note E, is the ability to believe and trust—in you, in others, in some spirituality greater than you. Faith fuels you to try again, to overcome struggles, to persevere, to be resilient. Faith is one's belief—"I'm OK as I am right NOW."

-Courage Wednesday, or the note F, is the ability to choose and to change—to act, to do the right thing, to decide, to choose a positive attitude, to try again and again and again. Courage chooses to change and to grow.

-Optimism Thursday, or the note G, is the ability to be positive in attitude and hopeful in outlook. Optimism is about how you look at things each moment—your view—through your attitude. Your attitude fuels hope for a future with a bright outcome.

-Kindness Friday, or the note A, is the ability to be patient and gentle—to respect, tolerate, acknowledge, accept, listen, and care. Kindness is self-kindness first. Kindness is patience and gentleness toward oneself and towards others.

-Charity Saturday, or the note B, is the ability to share and forgive. Charity is giving—sharing and revealing oneself to others—sharing one's feelings beyond thoughts and actions. Charity is forgiving yourself, letting go of the past, and forgiving others.

-Presence Everyday, or the note C, is the ability to breathe and be aware in the moment. Presence through active breathing—inhaling and exhaling—leads to awareness of one's thoughts, feelings, actions, and sensations—an outside observer engaged in the moment.

ASPIRE to Emotional Fitness. Live the NOW path, the SELF-ACCEPTANCE aim, the VALUES code, with ASPIRE energy. ASPIRE to Emotional Fitness and win the next five minutes with an ASPIRE attitude:

>   -aware-fully breathe and perceive – observe something with gratitude
>   -spiritually believe and trust – believe in something bigger than you
>   -physically choose and do – do something more than you
>   -intellectually form and talk – think of something positive about you
>   -relationally engage and connect – connect with something bigger than you
>   -emotionally feel and identify – feel something good about you

Dance the "think-feel-do" waltz of life now, in each moment. Find your personal zone of acceptance and of self-acceptance—to think, feel and do better. Ryan Edwards replayed the Playbook back in his mind—his portable framework to use as his character compass. He stood up and walked out of Room 101 feeling differently.

As Ryan exited the room, he stopped and noticed a plaque on the wall, the wall of Elise Matthews's homeroom. The plaque was a story—the starfish story. Ryan Edwards choked a little and drew closer to the plaque in order to read it.

CHAPTER 22

STARFISH STORY

"Life is for service."
Mister Rogers

Ryan began to read the starfish story by Loren Eiseley, "Once upon a time, there was a wise man who used to go to the ocean to do his writing. He had a habit of walking on to the beach before he began his work.

One day, as he was walking along the shore, he looked down the beach and saw a human figure moving like a dancer. He smiled to himself at the thought of someone who would dance to the day, and so, he walked faster to catch up.

As he got closer, he noticed that the figure was that of a young man, and that what he was doing was not dancing at all. The young man was reaching down the shore, picking up small objects, and throwing them into the ocean.

He came closer still and called out, 'Good morning! May I ask what it is that you are doing?'

The young man paused, looked up, and replied, 'Throwing starfish into the ocean.'

'I must ask, then, why you are throwing starfish into the ocean?' asked the somewhat startled wise man.

To this, the young man replied, 'The sun is up and the tide is going out. If I don't throw them in, they'll die.'

Upon hearing this, the wise man commented, 'But, young man, do you not realize that there are miles and miles of beach and there are starfish all along every mile? You can't possibly make a difference!'

At this, the young man bent down, picked up yet another starfish, and threw it into the ocean. As it met the water, he said, 'It made a difference for that one.'"

CHAPTER 23

REFLECTION

> "The greatest weapon against stress is our ability to choose one thought over another."
> **William James**

Ryan lost his breath. It all became crystal clear to him. Elise Matthews was the starfish thrower, Ryan's starfish thrower, and Ryan Edwards was the starfish. Elise Matthews specifically chose to save Ryan. She offered Ryan the notion that he could choose to free himself from his prison inside—with each exhale, each exhale of self-acceptance.

"Only you can free yourself from yourself, Mr. Edwards—only through self-acceptance. You have the keys to let yourself out of your self-imposed prison and jail sentence any time you decide. Choose to get out now with self-acceptance. The choice is yours.

"There are uncontrollable emotional waves in your life, like the waves of the ocean, that change each moment, adapting to the weather conditions and the tides of your setbacks and distress. Your feelings are your ocean waves and tides. Your thoughts and actions can help you avoid drowning in paralysis, procrastination, and unconscious emotion.

"There are layers of acceptance and self-acceptance, layers of peace, layers of joy to uncover throughout your life—living without doubt, fear, worry, doubt, judgment, opinion, interpretation, criticism, comparison, competition conclusion, or evaluation. Work toward acceptance, and self-acceptance, one layer at time.

"Acceptance is the safe place inside yourself where you are 'OK with yourself being just you.' It is your own emotional bunker and refuge. Return to your own self-acceptance.

"Fill the void, Mr. Edwards, with a self-accepting faith, belief, and trust, by surrendering and letting go. Fill the void with joy and peace—the joy and peace of self-acceptance.

Fun is a feeling—you feel it when you surrender, let go, stop fighting and controlling."

Ryan recalled Elise Matthews's final words that struck home, "If you want to be perfect, Mr. Edwards, then practice the PACE process and trust it, surrender to it, and let go of the outcome.

"If you want to be in control in the moment, then choose to control your attitude—choose to control your outlook, your disposition, your unconditional self-acceptance, your acceptance of others as they are, your acceptance of life as it is, your self-appreciation, your forgiveness of yourself, your forgiveness of others, your reaction to events, your response to situations, your thinking, your feeling, your doing, your values, your beliefs each moment . . . and let go of all the rest . . . because all the rest is out of your control."

CHAPTER 24

MAN IN MOTION—EIGHT DAYS A WEEK

> "A man cannot be comfortable without his own approval."
>
> Mark Twain

Ryan Edwards was a free man. No more lectures, no more assignments, no more deep thinking or feeling, no more difficult self-confrontation. Ryan was free or so he thought.

Ryan could not help but reflect on the eight meetings he had with Elise Matthews. She challenged him—a personal character challenge. He was skeptical of the playbook—the VALUES code, the ASPIRE energy, the SELF-ACCEPTANCE aim, the NOW path. What if the Playbook is true? What if the Emotional Athlete's PACE works after all? Ryan Edwards was experiencing a ferocious mental and emotional storm. He was totally undone since his time with Elise Matthews.

But now it was time to go back to life—football, girlfriend, friends, fun, and finally school. Ryan was going to go back to the way it was before Elise Matthews, stuffing her eight sessions in a locker. Or so he thought. Ryan couldn't find his way exactly back to the way it was before his eight meetings with Elise Matthews.

Ryan Edwards, the forty-nine year old Ryan Edwards, momentarily came out of his dream and returned to Matt's 2009 third-grade classroom. He was still deciding what he was going to say to the third-graders. It was a time warp for Ryan Edwards—all these memories he recalled in what seemed like only seconds. His reconnect with his son, Matt, and with Matt's classmates was but a brief return to the present day. Ryan was again drawn back to 1976, wandering back in time again for a few more flashbacks . . .

CHAPTER 25

Locker Room

> "Watch your thoughts; they become words. Watch your words; they become actions. Watch your actions; they become habit. Watch your habits; they become character. Watch your character; it becomes your destiny."
>
> Lao Tzu

Ryan was in the locker room after practice with his teammates on a Friday afternoon. Two of his friends, Robbie and Eric, were making fun of a third player, John. John was a nice guy. Ryan did not know him well. If anything John was a bit sensitive. So the routine harassment went on as it always had gone many times before.

Typically, Ryan would be party to it all, through silent amusement. He never joined in on insults towards John; however, he never stopped them either. He just watched it happen. Yet this time was a little different. This time Ryan Edwards realized that John wasn't happy with the abuse he constantly received and could do nothing about. For the first time ever it occurred to Ryan that the verbal abuse was wrong. The banter went on for a while and the temperature rose.

Robbie finally yelled, "John, you're just a fag. That's all there is to it."

With that comment, there was suddenly a pounding in Ryan's heart. What should he do? Normally, he had would have ignored Robbie's insult and offensive slur, as he had countless times in the past. However, Ryan was feeling out of sorts since his meetings with Elise Matthews. This time he knew that what was unfolding wasn't OK. So for the first time he engaged in the skirmish, "Robbie, knock it off."

Robbie snickered, "Oh, Ryan is the tough guy now."

Ryan repeated himself, "Robbie, knock it off."

With this retort, Robbie was now emboldened. All the other players were gathering around with interest. It appeared a new battle was unfolding.

Ryan stood his ground. This standoff had other social power implications too. Ryan was the quarterback, and Robbie was a star receiver. It was turning into a showdown. Typically, Ryan would try to smooth the situation over and move on. Ryan Edwards hated conflict and confrontation of any kind. But this time he wanted the bullying to stop, once and for all. "Robbie, don't do that again to John. Do you understand what I just said?"

Robbie was relishing this conflict. He was a star receiver and an instigator too. He did whatever he wanted because he could. "Ryan Edwards, you're just a pretty boy and not that tough. I can say what I want. John is a fag, let's face it."

In 1976, the idea of being gay was never discussed, only inferred. Unless of course you were labeling someone with a slur, as Robbie was labeling John.

Ryan became impatient. "Robbie, I will say it one last time. Stop it, and leave John alone, or you won't like where this ends up. I promise you."

Robbie started laughing loudly, and all the other teammates were joining Robbie's side as well. John was now watching, secretly delighted someone had finally come to his side. Robbie went for it. "John's a fag, that's all there is to it. And Ryan, you don't control anything around here. Back off."

Ryan Edwards was steamed but remained calm inside. This time, he could see the situation differently. It was almost as if he were stepping out of it himself and observing the conflict unfold while participating in it at the same time. "Robbie, I assure you that you won't like where this ends up." With that Ryan Edwards left the locker room to a chorus of banter. It seemed that Ryan Edwards had lost his team in that moment and that a mutiny had just occurred. It appeared that Robbie, the star receiver had won and was in charge now—at least for now.

CHAPTER 26

GAME ON

"A man is not hurt so much by what happens, as by his opinion of what happens."
Michel de Montaigne

The Fairfield High football game was the next afternoon. On the field, the game was tight. Fairfield was down by seven points in the second quarter. Ryan Edwards was completely off rhythm, and the team was not following him as it always had in the past. Yesterday's skirmish between Ryan and Robbie had taken a toll on Ryan's mental state and his standing among the team. Fairfield had the ball; it was second down and eight.

Ryan was calling a play. In the huddle, Robbie taunted Ryan, "Ryan, you OK? Did the 'fag' talk rattle you? Throw it to me; I'll take over and make you look good."

Ryan was stunned by Robbie's insubordination and abuse. The rest of the team watched in the huddle to see who would make the next move. Ryan remained cool. He then changed the play in his mind and called, "Post pattern left, to Robbie, on two."

Ryan broke the huddle and went up to the line to take the snap. He was undone but also stayed cool and composed at the same time. This "fag" talk was going to end and right now. Ryan would have ducked a confrontation, any and every confrontation, but not this time. He took the snap on two and dropped back three steps. Robbie, lined up on the right side, ran ten yard downfield and cut left on the crossing pattern as designed. Ryan set himself to pass and delivered it to Robbie.

But this was a very different pass. Ryan threw it two feet higher than normal. He never did that before given his outstanding ability and accuracy. Robbie saw it and was forced to jump higher than ever to catch the ball. He reached up and grabbed it. But the defenders were right there to undercut his legs and gave him a crushing series of hits. Robbie dropped to the ground and didn't get up. Cries came from the Fairfield stands.

The trainers came running on to the field. The officials called an injury time-out. Edwards trotted to the sidelines. Coach Thompson was livid, yelling at the top of his lungs to Ryan Edwards, "How could you throw that pass, Edwards! Robbie's hurt."

Ryan exhaled and said calmly, looking right into Coach Thompson's eyes, "Coach, I had to throw that pass. I just had to. Trust me. Put Smith in as his replacement. He is a sophomore, but he is eager and talented. I'll make him a star today."

With that Ryan ran back to the huddle. Coach Thompson was left speechless. He knew something was up, but also knew he would never really understand what went on with that last play. Back in the huddle all eyes were on Ryan Edwards. There was no longer any doubt who was in charge. Ryan Edwards was at the helm again after that pass to Robbie. Everyone knew what had happened.

Ryan's decision to throw that last pass two feet higher than normal ended the bullying. The rest of the team got the message. The bullying was over for good. Ryan set up Robbie for those ferocious hits. He made his statement to the team that the bullying was no longer tolerated and that there would be consequences for their actions if it happened again. Ryan gained a new respect by standing his ground on what he believed was right. Enough was enough. And he made sure that Robbie, and all the other players, knew it.

The game resumed, and there was a different tone. Ryan now led the team crisply on most every series throughout the rest of the game, adding three more scores. Ryan Edwards regained his poise and rhythm. Fairfield won easily. Smith, the sophomore replacement for Robbie, caught two touchdown passes and became an instant sensation. Robbie was out for at least three games due to an injury to his back.

And there would never be any more bullying in the locker room at Fairfield High. There were no more "fag" slurs from that moment forward toward John, or anyone else. The topic was never discussed again.

John cornered Ryan after the game. "Ryan, you didn't need to do that for me."

Ryan smiled softly. "John, I should have stepped in a long time ago, and I'm sorry I didn't." With that comment, Ryan Edwards left the locker room a new man. Ryan thought to himself that he had changed in a transforming way. Ryan wondered if Elise Matthews's Playbook had subconsciously played some small role in his decision in this incident.

Ryan was more assured and stronger about himself. He responded differently this time, making a tough decision based on his new set of values. He made a step forward too in his own self-acceptance with that last encounter with Robbie.

Standing up for what he believed, he didn't know whether it was Wednesday courage, Friday kindness, Sunday humility, Everyday presence, or some combination of them all that kicked in, guiding him through the conflict and his decision to stand up for John. It didn't matter. He was just pleased that this time he stayed true to himself, to his values, and to what he thought was right.

CHAPTER 27

HOMECOMING

> "The greatest discovery of my generation is that a human being can alter his life by altering his attitudes."
>
> **William James**

It was the Tuesday morning before homecoming, the second week of October. Ryan's girlfriend, Kate, the captain of the cheerleading squad and the 'femme fatale' of the senior class, was in the hallway with her friends. She was stunning, but she was also a bitch. She could do whatever she wanted, and she did, because she was good looking and had a body to match.

Before the first class, Ryan walked down the main hallway toward the girls' lockers and saw a scene unfolding. Kate and a few of her friends were talking in a catty way about another girl, Julie. Kate started first, "If Julie doesn't stick with the homecoming plan as I told her, I'll teach her a lesson. She's so homely, she can't even get a date for homecoming Saturday night."

Slowing his gait, Ryan cringed inside at what he was hearing from Kate. It felt like fingernails down the chalkboard for Ryan. Kate was cute, but she was also brutally mean at times. And this was one of those times. Once again, Ryan couldn't hold back. "Kate, what's going on?"

Kate answered, "Julie seems to think the homecoming dance should include a few changes. I didn't authorize them. She's not even going to the dance. I can't stand that pathetic girl. She drives me nuts. I'm not sure why anyone could be friends with her, anyway."

He was livid. He had had enough. Ryan Edwards, the new Ryan Edwards, paused, thought, but then couldn't hold back, "Kate, I am sure that people might say the same thing about you." In the past, Ryan would have tacitly smiled and let Kate's mean comments go unchallenged, as he had always done. But this time was different.

The girls all gasped. Kate turned red. She didn't hesitate and slapped Ryan in the face. Ryan did nothing. Typically, Kate verbally abused Ryan, as she did everyone else, when things didn't go her way. Kate then said, "Ryan, if you don't watch it, you won't be going to the homecoming dance with me."

Ryan broke into a slow and patient smile. Again, he didn't know what had come over him, but he wasn't going to tolerate Kate's physical slap or verbal punch this time. He knew that Kate was once again way out of line. For some reason, he was not going to take it this time. Ryan Edwards called Kate's bluff. "Kate, I have nothing to watch out for, and there won't be a next time. We won't be going the homecoming dance together, just as you suggested."

The girls were more stunned and showed it with their shocked expressions. Completely undone, Kate tried to back pedal. This had never happened to Kate before. Nobody would think of challenging her. She was always in control, or so she thought. "Ryan, you wouldn't dare. Don't make threats like that again or we won't be going out much longer."

Ryan had had enough, saying calmly, "Kate, that wasn't a threat. We are not going to the dance together. And I think that it may be a good idea of yours that we take a break."

Ryan confirmed to all in sight that he was not going to the homecoming dance with Kate, and that he had just broken up with his girlfriend of two years. With that, Ryan walked off to class. He wasn't sure what happened, on many levels, but he was clear that he did the right thing. He was sure that standing up for Julie and stopping the carnage that Kate typically inflicted on everyone else was the right thing to do.

Ryan Edwards was continuing to change. He stood up for what he believed was right for the second time now, after the locker room incident with Robbie. He wasn't sure if the PACE of life in the Playbook—ASPIRE NOW, VALUE SELF-ACCEPTANCE—was somehow kicking in. Nonetheless, he was sure that he did the right thing. For the first time, Ryan didn't care how others would look at it or what others thought of him and his actions.

The belief that he didn't need the approval of others was a new freedom for Ryan. This time, he didn't need the approval of others as a filter for his safe, non-confrontational behavior. He did what he thought was the right thing to do and merely acted accordingly. It was refreshing. It was freedom of a new kind.

CHAPTER 28

PIANO PRACTICE – SESSION 3

> "Nothing in the world can take the place of persistence. Talent will not; nothing is more common than unsuccessful men with talent. Genius will not; unrewarded genius is almost a proverb. Education will not; the world is full of educated derelicts. Persistence and determination alone are omnipotent. The slogan 'press on' has solved and always will solve the problems of the human race."
>
> **Calvin Coolidge**

Two days later Ryan was headed to the piano room. A few weeks had passed since Ryan Edwards's historic week of lectures by Elise Matthews. However, he had done little in the way of preparing for the December piano recital. He needed a piece to play. "Mary Had A little Lamb" sounded like a good idea right now.

It was Thursday afternoon, and he had a free period before football practice. A little nervous and not knowing why, he went to the music room, hoping to make a break through on his assignment but without any real plan.

As he entered, he heard the piano playing. It was Julie, playing a Mozart sonata. It was beautiful. Ryan paused looking at Julie. Ryan had not ever spent much time with Julie and didn't know her well. But as he watched her perform, he was struck by something new. Julie was anything but homely. She was really cute. But it was more than just Julie's looks. She was really nice.

As she sat there playing the piano, Ryan noticed that she had a calm and easy way about her. She seemed comfortable in her own skin—something Ryan unknowingly longed for all his life. But even with all of his accomplishments, Ryan Edwards was never enough for himself, and he never felt comfortable in his skin. This was the first time Ryan had ever stopped to think about that notion.

Julie was attractive in an entirely different manner. She was attractive from the inside out. Julie was attractive on the inside and on the outside. She saw Ryan and stopped playing. "Hi, Ryan, have you been there long," she said in a sweet and even more attractive voice.

Ryan was embarrassed. He said, "No, Julie, not too long. I came by to start on my piano project for the recital. I am going to blow it big-time if I don't figure this out."

Julie smiled reassuringly. "I'm sure you will come through as you always do."

Ryan then continued, "I had no idea that you played the piano so well. I never noticed before."

Julie responded, "Thanks, Ryan. I just love to play the piano as you do football."

Ryan then added, "I need to learn a piece. I have to pick one that I can play without making a fool out of myself at the December recital."

Julie then offered, "I can help you if you want. It's not that hard if you learn a few of the basics. I have time this weekend. I am not going to the homecoming dance."

Ryan made an admission to Julie as well, "Well, Julie, I am not going to the dance either. Kate and I broke up." Ryan Edwards was always a gentleman, even though he was self-absorbed. "It was her idea." Ryan clearly had broken up with Kate but was telling everyone that she had broken up with him. He was trying to save face for Kate, though he was still asking himself why he was doing so.

Julie was taken back. "I hadn't heard. I am sorry."

Ryan replied back, "Thanks, but I really need to find a song to play for the recital and get Elise Matthews off my back."

Julie reaffirmed, "Ryan, I'll help you, I have time Sunday. I will think about a piece for you to play. I may have one in mind that will get Elise Matthews's attention. It just might work and won't be too hard for you to learn."

Ryan seemed delighted for the first time with the project. "Thanks, Julie, that's great. I'll call you. Good seeing you."

"Sure Ryan," Julie responded. "Just call me."

With that Ryan started to walk out of the music room. Then something came over him, and he stopped and paused for a moment. He asked himself a question and answered, "why not?" Ryan then returned to the music room. Julie had restarted her practice. This time, he went up to the piano, and Julie stopped with a smile when she saw Ryan return.

Ryan was unusually nervous. "Julie, would you like to go the dance with me on Saturday night?"

Julie blushed. Never in her wildest dreams would she have thought that the star athlete and best-looking guy in the school would be asking her to the dance. Julie regained her composure. "Ryan, I would be delighted to go with you. Thank you."

Ryan exhaled deeply with great relief and the understanding that he had not been rejected again. Then he smiled confidently again, "Great, I will pick you up at 6:30 p.m. Julie, this will be fun!"

With that Ryan Edwards walked out of the piano room one more time. All the while he was increasingly struck by the idea that Julie was really cute and that the more he spoke to her, the more attracted he had become. She was nice. He wondered why he had never been able to see this before. This was going to be a great homecoming dance after all. He just knew it inside.

CHAPTER 29

December Recital

> "No one can make you feel inferior without your consent."
>
> **Eleanor Roosevelt**

Ryan Edwards had been practicing the piano three times a week since the homecoming dance. It didn't hurt that his new girlfriend, Julie, was training him regularly. Since that last encounter in October when Ryan took a risk and invited Julie to the homecoming dance, Ryan had never been happier. Julie was the best girlfriend Ryan had ever known.

Ryan also continued to wrestle with all that Elise Matthews had taught him. He was trying out the Playbook from all different angles to see how the principles could possibly apply to his life. He was practicing them in different ways, in different scenarios, again and again. Something new was happening. Ryan Edwards was changing, transforming, getting better, and feeling happier all at the same time. He was working his new Playbook that Elise Matthews had customized for him. He discovered through practice what worked for him and applied it in real life.

His thinking improved too. His destructive negative thoughts were replaced with more realistic and supportive notions about himself. His healthier, more positive thinking patterns positively affecting his feelings, which he now noticed. His upbeat thinking and improved feeling also affected his doing. He performed better in every way with less effort, less anxiety, and more enjoyment. The think-feel-do triangle offense was beginning to work for Ryan Edwards in an effortless and flowing way.

At the outset in October, Julie was just a nice girl. But she became cuter and prettier as he got to know her better. Ryan Edwards even started to enjoy the piano. Their time together through piano practice was becoming a fun activity they shared in common.

It was now the evening of the recital. Ryan Edwards was prepared and practiced. He was nervous. He hoped he would do well for Elise Matthews. He wanted to show Elise his appreciation—his deep appreciation and gratitude to her—through this performance.

The evening progressed, and it would soon be Ryan Edwards's turn to perform. The moment finally arrived, and Ryan went up to the stage when called. He stood silently in front of the microphone for a few seconds before starting.

Elise Matthews was seated three quarters of the way back in the auditorium packed with students and parents, though not Ryan Edwards's parents. This recital was the students' show. Elise was only an observer at this point, no longer the teacher. She, too, was nervous with growing anticipation. What piece would Ryan Edwards perform? Oh, please let him perform OK and not embarrass himself, she thought.

Ryan adjusted the microphone and introduced himself. "Good evening, I'm Ryan Edwards. First I would like to thank Miss Matthews for all her instruction. It was more than I had ever bargained for. Tonight I would like to play the first section of 'Fur Elise' by Beethoven." "Fur Elise" meant "For Elise" in German. Beethoven wrote the piece for a sweetheart he had hoped to marry. Ryan Edwards was playing Beethoven's "Fur Elise" for Elise Matthews.

Elise Matthews's heart stopped. She was paralyzed in fear, respect, admiration, courage, and a whole host of other feelings she couldn't quite identify. What about "Mary Had a Little Lamb?" Beethoven's "Fur Elise" was a fairly difficult number, even with a beginners' piano arrangement. Julie had picked a fairly basic arrangement for him and helped Ryan master it. Elise was puzzled until she made the connection that Julie, the piano virtuoso and Ryan's girlfriend, had coached him through it all. Elise was deeply touched.

Ryan seated himself and adjusted his position at the piano. Clearly, Ryan knew what to do. Julie had meticulously trained and coached Ryan since they started going out in October. He confidently paused before beginning. Ryan began playing "Fur Elise" for Elise Matthews.

Elise Matthews began cry, hiding it from everyone. She knew that Ryan Edwards chose to play "Fur Elise" for her. Ryan was playing the first section reasonably well, with some mistakes. But for the first time ever, Ryan Edwards was feeling OK with not being perfect. He was OK with his mistakes on stage, all the while saying at the same time, "Thank you, Miss Matthews—for everything."

After the December recital, Ryan Edwards continued to practice rigorously and use the Playbook as often as he could. He worked with it, tested it, and through trial and error, came to learn what worked for him and what didn't. From the recital on, Ryan practiced the plays in the Playbook with a daily discipline and repetition right through to graduation, and it showed.

Ryan was trying, and growing, and changing. Through the Playbook, he learned that he could often influence the attitude of others by the attitude he displayed himself. And his attitudes were getting better—starting with his attitude of self-acceptance, and accepting things as they occur and other people as they are. His thinking improved his feeling, which improved his doing. Think-feel-do.

As he became more aware of himself through his experiences and his awareness in his surroundings, Ryan continued to add to his insights with each new experience. He learned what worked for him and what didn't, as he slowly came out from inside himself. He engaged more in the external world with others and with life itself—forgetting himself through self-acceptance.

CHAPTER 30

GRADUATION

> "A man is what he thinks about all day long."
> Ralph Waldo Emerson

Ryan Edwards had just graduated with his classmates at the Fairfield commencement ceremony, but he had two good-byes to say—to his two most influential coaches at Fairfield High School. He first stopped by Elise Matthews's campus house and knocked on her door.

Elise Matthews opened the door with a smile, holding some flowers in a vase with one hand. Ryan smiled while observing the description tag on the flowers. Ryan Edwards had come a long way since last September, growing and maturing in emotional ways she had never imagined. Elise was the first to speak, "Hello, Ryan," using no last name this time, personally and warmly.

Ryan smiled back with a self-effacing, self-assured, somewhat humble smile, "Hello, Miss Matthews. I wanted to say good-bye and thank you. I also want to say that you may be the toughest and the prettiest coach I have ever had. I will remember your music class."

Elise

Elise Matthews almost blushed. She told herself she was much too old for that. "Well, thank you, Ryan. You had quite a year. I will enjoy following your successes in the fall."

Ryan had a wrapped box for Elise. "I have a present for you."

Elise took it from Ryan with a sense of surprise. She opened it, and smiled. It was a handwritten journal by Ryan with the name "The Playbook," on the cover. Inside were the notes, comments and conversations she and Ryan had had last fall. They included the chalk-talk blackboard writings Elise Matthews drew up on that second Sunday morning of the 7:00 a.m. extra sessions.

Elise Matthews sighed with immense gratitude. "Ryan, thank you." She had no idea that Ryan had taken that week of eight extra sessions so seriously or that he had taken the time afterward to write down his own notes about their meetings. Ryan made two copies of the Playbook—one for Elise and one for himself.

As Ryan went up to hug Elise Matthews, he hesitated, but then, unconcerned about propriety or appearances, kissed Elise on the cheek.

Elise Matthews blushed again before recoiling and regained herself so that she didn't cry. Elise Matthews had somewhat fallen for Ryan Edwards in her own way. Yet knowing that they were worlds and ages apart, she was aware that they most likely would never meet again.

This would be the second time Elise Matthews would find herself alone. The last time was three years ago when she lost the love of her life, Jeff Wilson. She had shut him out. Elise Matthews had always performed her way—emotionally shut down—through every relationship, as she did in every aspect of her life. She kept her distance from others and from Jeff, never letting anyone get too close to know her.

Elise Matthews blew it three years ago with Jeff. He left her and found someone else. He was now married. Elise still thought about it often. So Elise Matthews came to Fairfield last fall for a fresh start.

Elise Matthews didn't want anyone—least of all Ryan Edwards—to make her same mistake. That's why Elise Matthews, when Ryan Edwards selected the piano as his recital instrument, chose Ryan Edwards as her starfish. She would throw him back into the ocean and try to save him. Elise didn't want Ryan to make the same mistakes of keeping people at a distance, never sharing, never letting anyone in, and trying to go it alone in life without asking anyone for help.

While protecting Ryan, Elise always had Jeff Wilson in the back of her mind, the lost love of her life. Elise had lived and acted as Ryan had lived and acted that first September school day last fall. She was in many ways just like Ryan—good looking, smart, athletic, popular, and completely isolated from herself and from others. And like Ryan, Elise did not let people inside.

Elise had a Fort Knox-like security system, full of impenetrable walls guarding her emotions, feelings, and deepest thoughts. Elise Matthews affirmed her way and performed her way through life, in an attempt to block out all sense of her feelings. She was afraid to share herself and let other people into her life. Elise Matthews would "do" her way through all situations without ever feeling anything along the way.

Afraid for Ryan, Elise did not want him to make the same mistakes—Elise Matthews became a starfish thrower, Ryan Edwards's starfish thrower. Ryan Edwards was the starfish, Elise Matthews's starfish.

Elise Matthews would never know for sure to what extent she had influenced Ryan Edwards's life—his emotional life. But she had a hunch that she made a real difference.

Elise

Ryan waved good-bye as he walked away from Elise Matthews's house. He looked back at Elise one more time. As he did, he noticed that even more than her stunning looks Elise Matthews had kind eyes—kind eyes that made you feel OK being you just as you were when in her presence. Elise Matthews had kind, beautiful and accepting eyes.

Ryan Edwards ran off to one final stop before leaving Fairfield High for the last time as a student. Ryan's next visit was with Coach Thompson. He jogged over to the field where he could always find his coach.

Ryan ran up to him, thanked him, and gave him a strong hug. On the way off the field, Ryan turned and for the first time gave a direction to Coach Thompson. "Coach, go home, take a shower, put on a blazer, buy some flowers, and ask Elise Matthews out on a date."

Coach Thompson chuckled, paused, grinned, and yelled back, "Yes sir, Mr. Edwards."

"And she likes peonies," Ryan added as he left.

Coach Thompson yelled back, "Edwards, now how do you know that?"

Ryan Edwards turned back one more time with a smile. "Coach, I noticed."

CHAPTER 31

BACK AT MATTHEW'S CLASS

> "I am still determined to be cheerful and happy, in whatever situation I may be; for I have also learned from experience that the greater part of our happiness or misery depends upon our dispositions, and not upon our circumstances."
>
> Martha Washington

Suddenly, Ryan Edwards was startled out of his flashbacks to senior year in high school. Miss Wright interrupted Ryan from his reverie, "Mr. Edwards, are you all right?"

Ryan regained his composure. Lost in space and flashbacks to 1976 at Fairfield High School, for what seemed like hours he said, "Oh, I am fine, Miss Wright. Thank you."

Ryan decided what he was going to say, taking a different approach—one he made up then and there. "Boys and girls, it is true, I am a businessman. However, I think I can explain what I do in another way for you. I would like to tell you a story. Have any of you ever heard of the starfish story?"

None had. All of the children shook their heads no.

"Well, it is a fine story," Ryan replied. "Let me tell it to you from memory as best I can." Ryan retold the starfish story, as he had done many times over the years. He knew it easily from memory.

Ryan then described himself. "I am a businessman but really more of a coach—an emotional trainer and coach. I teach people to help themselves get better. I help them grow and recover from their emotional injuries. Like a personal trainer helps a person get physically fit through endurance, strength, and flexibility physical training, I help people become emotionally fit through emotional training—through self-acceptance training.

"When you are emotionally fit, life seems a little bit easier—how you think, how you feel, and how you do things. Everyday is a workout day—an emotional workout day, just like your physical workout day when you go to recess."

One of the kids raised his hand and asked, "Where's your office?"

Ryan Edwards responded, "It's at 'The Gym,' that's the name of my office. People come to The Gym for an Emotional Fitness workout."

Another child followed up, "What is emotionally fit?"

Ryan smiled. "Emotional Fitness is a lifelong journey toward self-acceptance. It is merely being on your own side—all the time, in good times or bad times. It is being one's own best friend, being OK with being you just as you are. Being on one's own side is about self-acceptance, right now, being OK being who you are as you are. You're already OK."

Ryan Edwards was on roll. He sounded like Elise Matthews had sounded to him in their eight sessions in the fall of 1976. "When you can accept yourself as you are, the mental noise in your head tends to diminish. The doubt, the fear, the worry, the anxiety, the obsessing, the compulsions, the procrastinating, the distressing, the ruminating, the downing, the regretting, the guilt, the shaming, the perfecting, the condemning—all lessen."

Ryan Edwards was totally unaware of his passionate argument. If he were able to stop and step back from the moment, he might have realized that he was doing to Matt's classmates what Elise Matthews had once done to him in the fall of 1976. But he couldn't help himself. His passion to help relieve the pain of being one's own worst enemy was all consuming. Ryan Edwards wanted to help anyone who might listen. With self-acceptance, there is more willingness and an ability to want to change and grow as a person.

"With self-acceptance in the moment, life tends to feel and go a little better. With self-acceptance, there is self-compassion, self-tolerance, self-empathy, self-patience, self-trust, self-confidence, self-esteem, self-respect, and self-appreciation.

"Surrender yourself, be who you are. Let go of self-protecting, self-preserving masks and mirrors. Life becomes easier. Distorting, posturing, exaggerating, approval seeking diminish.

"Being an 'Emotional Athlete' requires you 'Think To Cope' emotionally and behaviorally to be OK—to know you are OK being just you as you are.

"It means trying to be nice to yourself, a little more each day. That's the essence of kindness—that's self-kindness. Be nice to yourself. You'll be nicer to other people. How you think about yourself determines how you think about and accept life and accept others.

"This is the essence of faith—faith in being nice to yourself. And that faith comes from believing that you are OK as you are and then trusting that belief.

"You, boys and girls, are already there. Your challenge is to stay there and not lose what you already have in its innocence and purity. Being in a hurry to be an adult is overrated.

"For adults the goal is to get back to the beginning to see the simplicity of it all—the simplicity of being a child—being OK just being you. The simplicity is lost when we strive to be adults. Continue to be you as you are. Breathe, exhale, and smile through life.

"Be a child—without judgment, interpretation, comparison, competition, opinion, evaluation, self-monitoring or second guessing.

"Be a child—with pure innocence and acceptance that I'm OK, it's OK, you're OK, it will be OK. That's the place to be. And you are there right now.

"'Being OK being me' is the one gift you can always give to yourself.

"Are you a shrink?" another kid asked. All the kids laughed.

"No, I'm just a helper. Nobody wants to be called a shrink, but everyone wants to help."

Ryan paused. "And that's what I do." With that Ryan Edwards stopped. He recalled the image of the plaque on the wall of Elise Matthews's homeroom, Room 101 and said, "So even though you might call me a businessman or a coach, I would prefer you think of me as a 'starfish thrower.'"

All the boys and girls just giggled. Then one of Matt's classmates, Taylor, asked, "Mr. Edwards, how does one become a starfish thrower?" The children laughed again, this time even louder.

Ryan Edwards smiled with a very broad and fun smile. "Great question. To become a starfish thrower, you often start out as a starfish. You may be thrown back into the sea by an older, wiser starfish thrower."

The children were amused and captivated. Another child, Jack, asked, "Then what?"

Ryan Edwards paused, a very long pause, and smiled again. "After the starfish has been thrown back into the ocean a few times, it may recognize in gratitude its good fortune. Sometimes, a starfish is thrown back once. In my case, since I am a little stubborn, I was a starfish that was thrown back into the ocean several times. Most of the time, I didn't know I was even being thrown back into the ocean."

Ryan caught his breath and continued, "A starfish thrower walking up and down the beach has his pick of thousands of starfish to throw back into the water. One particular starfish thrower chose me. I was the lucky starfish chosen one day, Tuesday the 5th of September, 1976."

Ryan Edwards picked up momentum, "You may decide to become a starfish thrower yourself one day and help others in need. You may 'search the beach,' you may spot a helpless starfish, you may want to throw the starfish back in the water, and you may throw it back in as best you can."

The children were spellbound—both by the story itself and by the fact that Ryan Edwards, though talking to the children, appeared to be lost in space, lost in his thoughts.

Miss Wright interjected, "Boys and girls, one final question for Mr. Edwards. Matthew, perhaps you have one for your dad."

Matthew thought earnestly and then asked, "Dad, who was your starfish thrower?"

With that question, Matt struck a chord in his father's heart. He thought and then replied to his son, "Elise, Elise Matthews, my senior year music teacher in high school." A tear came down Ryan Edwards's cheek. "Elise Mathews was my starfish thrower. Thanks for inviting me today."

At that point the third graders laughed and giggled and clapped for Ryan Edwards. Matt Edwards was very proud of his dad. He was relieved with the thought that his dad's story was more interesting than he ever imagined it to be. Ryan Edwards did not embarrass his son.

Matt walked his dad out of school, "Thanks, Dad. You were better than I thought you'd be."

Ryan Edwards smiled. "Thanks, Matt. I am glad I didn't disappoint you or your classmates."

Ryan Edwards walked to his car and smiled again, reflecting on the hour at Matt's school.

More importantly, Ryan was thinking about high school and about Elise Matthews. Where was she now? He thought about her as he drove back to work, back to The Gym.

Elise Matthews taught music at Fairfield High School for thirty years after her initial year with Ryan. And she did marry, not the football coach, but the new headmaster who came to Fairfield High five years later. Elise continued teaching piano actively to young students after she and her husband moved on from Fairfield High.

The Gym became a nationwide network of Emotional Fitness centers to teach high school and college students how to cope with life's challenges through Emotional Fitness training, starting with self-acceptance. The Gym developed and trained Emotional Athletes.

Ryan started The Gym based on The Playbook principles that Elise Matthews had scratched out on the blackboard in September of 1976. The eight Playbook sessions turned out to be some of the most influential chalk talks Ryan ever received from any coach, mentor, teacher, or friend.

The Gym expanded to people of all ages who—through their own self-acceptance—were willing and able to make changes in their emotional lives.

ASPIRE to Emotional Fitness—aware-fully, spiritually, physically, intellectually, relationally, and emotionally—become an Emotional Athlete. The athletes who train at The Gym commit to change and to Emotional Fitness in their lives—they decide to become Emotional Athletes through self-acceptance.

The Emotional Athlete's PACE towards self-acceptance leads to Emotional Fitness—ASPIRE NOW, VALUE SELF-ACCEPTANCE.

The Gym developed an emotional handicap system to track one's progress. The handicap system worked in golf, so Ryan tried an emotional handicap system at The Gym.

A golfer goes to the golf course and has the pro look at his swing to improve his game. So why wouldn't someone go to an emotional pro to look at his emotional swing to improve his emotional game?

Why not have a pro take a look at someone's emotional swing—whether a 20-handicap or a 5-handicap emotionally? Why the stigma around mental health and Emotional Fitness? Why wouldn't you go see your emotional pro and ask for help in your emotional game—toward greater self-acceptance, toward greater acceptance of others, and toward greater acceptance of life as it comes? Why wouldn't you?

Ryan Edwards spent thirty years refining the Playbook for The Gym based on the Think To Cope belief. How you think drives how you feel, and how you feel motivates what you do. Think-feel-do. He remembered the eight values by the eight days of the week and by the notes of the C major scale—always remembering at the same time the best coach in his life—Elise Matthews, his starfish thrower.

Ryan Edwards thanked Elise Matthews one more time in his mind for being his starfish thrower and changing his life forever. Calling his wife, Ryan left a voice mail message, "Honey, Matt will keep me as his dad. I am going to The Gym. I'll be home at seven."

With that, Ryan Edwards ended the call and went to his favorite place and passion, where he always loved to practice and work out each and every day—The Gym.

EPILOGUE:

"Fall down seven times, stand up eight."
                                    Japanese proverb

Con, Hay, Row, Tug-

Keep going…

Dad

The End

Edwards Brothers Malloy
Thorofare, NJ USA
August 21, 2014